A Howl for Help

JK Brandon

The Howl Series:

A Howl in the Night
The Twilight Howl
A Howl for Help

www.ahowlinthenight.com

A Howl for Help copyright © 2012 by Jerry Brandon

Cover art copyright © 2012 by Jerry Brandon

ISBN-13 978-1481165259
ISBN-10 1481165259

PRELUDE...

One cold December night, outside in the desert.

The injured dog lay for two days, resting and licking his leg. Every time he tried to stand it hurt too much, so his innate canine sense told him to hole-up and wait. The nights were cold, but he snuggled in the dead grass and thin leaves under an overgrown Arizona desert tree and found the warmth his short-hair coat wouldn't provide.

On the third day his leg hurt less than his stomach, and his concern switched to food and water. Somehow he knew if he stayed there any longer he might never get up. He rose on three weak legs and steadied himself, then started toward distant house lights, leaving the safety of the weeping Mesquite that had been his refuge. He moved away from the bordering highway, away from the cars and the trucks and the speeding drivers.

He hobbled east through open desert, paralleling the mountains until he smelled water nearby. He sniffed out a small rain puddle in a rocky wash and lapped desperately at the cold liquid. Soon he felt better, but he was still weak and needed food.

Just then a rabbit burst from under a bush and startled him. He jumped back in shock, yelping from the pain from straining his rear leg. He stood a moment, then focused on his immediate need.

Food.

Humans had food. He had to find humans.

He eyed the line of houses bordering the desert, staring into the backyards with a touch of sadness for his lost master. It had been days now, and he'd grown skittish from living as a stray. He didn't know if he'd ever see his human again.

He moved along behind the houses, then stopped hopefully, smelling some uneaten dog food in a pet dish. He searched for an opening into the backyard but found none. He thought momentarily about digging under the fence, but his rear leg hurt too much for that.

His hopes were dashed when a small Pomeranian burst through the house dog door and ran close, barking furiously at him through the open bars of the metal fence. He backed up and limped on; aware he couldn't be attacked but saddened by his rejection. He kept moving further across the desert, staying away from the houses and unfriendly dogs.

He'd traveled about a half-mile through cactus and scrub brush when suddenly the bright lights of a two-story house drew his attention. Something about this home made him stop. He looked through the iron fence into the back yard, searching for clues to his feeling. He should have felt wary. He smelled dogs, two dogs that lived there, but for some reason he did not feel unwelcome at this home. He moved closer to the fence.

It wasn't food that drew him closer, it was hope. He felt safe at this brightly-lit house. He forgot his hunger but not his dilemma. The injured dog needed help and hoped he could find it there, but he was feeble and vulnerable to attack.

He was twenty feet from the backyard view fence. He hesitated, but then took a chance. He had to let his presence be known. A sound pushed out his throat, a sound part cry and part howl, a sound he'd never heard before or knew he could utter.

awwwoooooawwoooooooooo.

It was weak but desperate, like the wounded dog who cried out. He waited, then he called for help again.

awwwoooooawwoooooooooo.

It was his last hope.

ONE

One cold December night, inside a warm house.

My ears twitched at the strange sound coming from out back. I cocked my head, unsure of what I'd just heard. I turned to my buddy sprawled on the living room rug.

"You hear that, Meat?"

Meatloaf woke and raised his head. "I didn't hear anything."

That didn't surprise me. Meatloaf could sleep through anything, except maybe the rustling of a new dog food bag being opened.

"Outside," I said. "I thought I heard a dog cry, a dog out back."

He sighed and stretched his legs straight out until they shook. "There's no dogs out in the desert, Taser. Just snakes and coyotes. It's probably the wind."

"Yeah," I said. "Probably. There's no dogs out in the desert."

I didn't move to investigate, but I left one ear up. If it was a dog, it wasn't any mutt I knew. The dogs around our neighborhood were snug in their homes, full from dinner but hopin' for leftovers—if they were lucky.

Meatloaf and I weren't hangin' around the dinner table, though. Robert, our master was out for the evening, out for dinner with a female—but there was always a chance of a doggie bag.

Then I thought I heard it again. I stood and walked to the dog door. Maybe it was nothing, but I had to check it out. I'm not nosy, it's my job. It was my house, it was my neighborhood.

By the way, I'm Taser. Meatloaf and I are Labs.

Black Labradors.

Funny business is our business, we watch this neighborhood, nothin' gets by us.

Nothin' gets by me, anyway. Meatloaf, well…

I was only halfway to the rear fence when I smelled a dog out there, out beyond our yard. He needed a bath, yeah, but that wasn't it. He smelled scared, but not dangerous.

I moved closer to the view fence, curious and concerned.

"Woof," I barked. Friendly like. Not challenging. "Who are you?" I asked.

"My name is Whiskey," the dog said. "Or it was, when I had a master."

I walked right up to the fence bars. I could make out his thin outline in the dim light. He looked to be a mix, mostly Pointer, with a white and brown coat.. When my eyes adjusted I could see he was older, seven or eight. He had a sad but friendly face. Skinny, I thought. He looked like he could use a good meal.

"I'm so hungry," he said simply. "Do you have any scraps of food I could eat?"

He moved closer to the fence, hobbling on three legs.

I stared at him. "What happened to your back leg?" The sight of his tucked-up rear paw shocked me.

"I was in an accident."

"A car?"

"Yeah, a car hit me. A whisker closer and I could have been killed."

I examined the leg he held up close to his body. "Does it hurt?"

"Yes, but not as much as it did," he said. "But I'm weak from no food."

"Of course, I'm sorry. I'll get you something, wait here."

I ran back inside and thought about what I could bring. I could get to the dog bag because we were on the honor system with Robert here, but it would be hard to take him loose dog food nuggets. I went in the pantry and scanned the shelves. All the pantry shelves we could reach had food cans or sealed boxes on them. Robert usually put the good stuff higher so Meatloaf wouldn't be tempted. But I thought there might be something I could get to.

9

I put my front paws on a shelf, stood on my hind legs and looked on the upper shelves.

Yes!

A half-loaf of wheat bread sat waiting for me. I bit into the soft wrapper and pulled it down quietly, hoping Meatloaf wouldn't hear what I was doin'. I snuck back out the dog door with it in my jaws. The fence bars were just wide enough to poke the bread through.

"Take it," I said.

He pulled it over to his side and ate hungrily, eating even the plastic bag. I watched him chew until the food was all gone. He licked the crumbs on the ground.

"Where do you live?" I asked him.

He looked up at me, licking his lips. "Nowhere, now. I'm a stray."

I wanted to let him know that didn't have to be permanent. "I was a stray for a while, on the westside. Then I got thrown in the pound."

"I been to the pound. I don't want to go back there," he said.

"Can't blame ya for that."

I knew all about the county dog pound. It was a rough world.

"I can live on my own," he said.

I wasn't sure that was true, especially with his bad leg. "But, what happened to your master?"

He hesitated. "I'm…I'm not sure."

I figured he didn't want to talk about it, so I left it alone.

He motioned toward the highway. "I got hit crossing that road. I stayed under a tree until I felt better."

I didn't want to say anything, but I knew coyotes were out there looking for a meal. This pooch was lucky. "So, where will you go now?" I asked.

"I don't know." He looked left and right. "Maybe I'll go back to my tree to get well. I just need more time."

"Look." I had to tell him. "It's dangerous out in that desert. You have to be careful, there's snakes and coyotes…" I didn't finish.

His head jerked up. "No! I'm…I'm too weak to fight a coyote."

I tried to think of something to help. He had to get out of that desert and into our subdivision. "There's a park not far, at the end of our street. If you keep going the way you were, you'll come to a big drainage pipe. Can you meet me there? I bet there's a safe place to hide in the park."

"Yes, I can meet you. Thank you."

I backed up. "Go now, I'll find you at the park."

Whiskey struggled on his way, hopping pitifully on one back leg.

I ran back in the house and checked on my pal. Meatloaf was still asleep, so I went to the side yard gate and flipped the latch to open it up. Robert had given up on tryin' to keep me in the backyard, but I needed to be careful not to be seen. If old man Crenshaw saw me, I'd be in trouble.

Crenshaw is the new head of the homeowner association, and he thinks he's the neighborhood alpha dog or somethin', which he ain't, because I'm the alpha dog around here.

I stuck my nose out front and looked. Nobody was walking around, it was mealtime for most people home from work. I took off running to the park. It was only three houses away. Besides, I'm black and I blend well into the night, but I was worried about neighbors telling Crenshaw I'd snuck out again.

The park was empty so I went right to the drainage pipe, but I didn't see the injured dog. Could a coyote have gotten him already? I felt guilty, like I should have done more.

I called out in the night. "Whiskey!"

I heard nothing in reply. I ran through the pipe and out in the desert, then I saw him hobbling slowly toward me. I saw instantly that he was no match for any coyote who wanted to attack him.

I called again. "Whiskey!"

He came over and stood. "Sorry, I had to stop and rest."

I pointed with my snout at the pipe opening. "Let's go in the park."

Once inside, standing on the park grass, I saw the problem. There was no place to for the stray to hide without being seen. The grass-

11

shortening people had trimmed all the trees and bushes so much that Whiskey couldn't stay out of sight. Someone would report him to the animal control people and he'd be off to the pound.

He looked around, and he must have seen the same problem. "It's all open space. Maybe my tree would be better."

I couldn't let him risk going back there, not with all the predators hunting at night. "No way, it's too dangerous."

"But…"

"No," I said firmly. I had an idea that might work. "You're coming home with me. I'll hide you at our place, in my dog house. I can bring you food out there every day. You can stay until you get better."

He looked worried. "But your master…"

I shook my snout. "I've got a dog house out back I don't use. Robert never looks in there. I'll explain it to my buddy Meatloaf, he won't care."

I wasn't too sure about that last part. I wasn't too sure about that first part either, but I had to chance it. What's the big deal if we get caught anyway? So Robert shakes his finger at me and says, *No, No, Bad Dog!* I hear that a lot anyway.

I pointed the way home. "Come on, it's not far."

Off we went, with me thinkin' it was a great plan. I couldn't think of a thing that could go wrong.

TWO
Refuge at Taser's house

We eased through the open fence gate, then I bit a piece of the wood slat and pulled it closed.

"Back here," I said.

I showed him my plastic dog house in the backyard. It was big and wide; Whiskey could move toward the back and stay out of sight. It was considered my dog house because Meatloaf wouldn't go in there. It was his issue about plastic not being natural materials, or something.

Whiskey looked it over. "This is wonderful, are you sure it's alright?"

"Sure. This is my house as much as Robert's. Stay here, I'll get my buddy and introduce you."

I went in the house to find Meatloaf. He was still holding the rug down in the living room, but his eyes were open.

"Meat. I need to tell you somethin'."

He lifted his head. "What now?"

"There's a stray in our back yard."

"A stray cat? So chase him away, I'm too tired."

"No, Meat, this is a dog, a guest of ours. I invited this dog to stay with us until he gets well, because he hurt his leg."

Meatloaf sat up and got this serious look on his face. "Are you crazy? We can't take in animals."

"His name is Whiskey."

"That's nice, but there's no room for three dogs in this house."

"We gotta hide him from Robert. I thought he could stay outside in my dog house."

13

"Oh great." Meatloaf thought a while. "I hope he's not allergic to plastic."

"Meat, nobody's allergic to plastic, that's why it's good stuff."

"Plastic causes cancer."

I ignored him. "Just for a week or two, until his leg heals."

"Birth defects, too."

"I'll share my food with him."

"You're gonna get us in trouble, Taser. I don't like it."

"He really needs our help."

Meatloaf looked at me like he was thinking, but I wasn't fooled. "What happened to his leg?" he asked.

"He got hit by a car."

"That's terrible. Wait, we have to feed him, too? There's not enough food around here now."

Meat was about ten pounds overweight, maybe more. But he didn't seem to think his weight was a problem. "Have some compassion, buddy," I said.

"We're not talking about compassion here, we're talking about basic canine survival."

"Come out and meet him."

"Alright, but I'm telling you, I got a bad feeling about this."

Meatloaf rose and followed me out to the dog house. Whiskey was already settled in, lying down with his head on his paws. He looked up when we appeared.

I nodded at our guest. "Whiskey, this is Meatloaf. He lives here with me and Robert."

Whiskey looked embarrassed. "I'm sorry to trouble you, but I really appreciate your help."

Meatloaf looked him over carefully. "What's with all your ribs showing? Are you a vegan?"

Whiskey cocked his head. "What's a vegan?"

I jumped in to explain. "Vegans are people from Vega."

"Vega? I don't know what that is."

"It's a city in California," I explained. "Nobody who lives there eats very much."

"I'm not a vegan," Whiskey said. "I'll eat anything, even garbage."

Meatloaf still didn't get it. "So your master put you on a diet?"

"No, I've been a stray, I don't eat very often. Just what I can find on the street."

Meatloaf shook his head. "Dog, you need a good meal. When's the last time you ate?"

"Well, I just had that bread Taser gave me."

"What bread?"

"Some whole wheat bread."

"What!" Meatloaf looked at me with horror. "You gave him the whole-wheat bread from our pantry? I had my eye on that."

I nodded. "Sorry. Whiskey needed it more than you."

"Maybe, but now I'm gonna hafta take the rap for that. Robert always blames me when food disappears."

"That's because you're always to blame."

He paused. "That may or may not be true."

"Quit complainin'." I turned to our new friend. "Don't worry about anything, Whiskey, just rest up. I'll check on you later, but Meat and I need to go inside and wait for Robert to get home."

"Thank you." Whiskey put his head back down and closed his eyes. I figured he must have been exhausted.

I nudged Meatloaf and we went back in the house. It seemed about time for our human to show up, and we had to do the faithful-dog-waiting-by-the-front-door-thing, otherwise he'd know we were up to something bad in the backyard. We lay down in the hallway close to the entry.

"Wow," said Meatloaf. "Whiskey looks terrible."

"Kinda makes you thankful for all we have."

It's not like we didn't know what it was like to be out on your own, both of us had lost homes and masters before. I'd been a stray and spent time in the dog pound before Robert rescued me. Meatloaf used to live in California, and he'd had a couple different masters.

"Too bad we don't have a swimming pool, Whiskey could take a bath," Meatloaf said. "What is he, a mix?"

"Looks like mostly a short-haired Pointer."

"Really?" Meatloaf raised one ear. "What color is he?"

"Mostly white, with big brown ears. Why?"

Meatloaf thought before he spoke, which was unusual. "Ahh…nothing. Probably just a coincidence."

"No come on."

"It's something Winston told me about a Pointer involved in something…"

He stopped talking when a key rattled in the door and Robert stepped in holding…yes! A doggie bag. We ran up and attacked his legs playfully while he reached down to pet us.

Hi Guys, he said.

Meatloaf had his nose on the bag as we walked down the hall into the kitchen. Robert put it on the counter while we sat at attention. He looked down at us and spoke.

It's a hamburger, but you already know that.

Our tails switched back and forth in a frenzy. Yeah, we already knew that. Drool leaked out of Meatloaf's mouth and hung halfway to the floor.

Honestly, Meatloaf can be embarrassing.

Robert looked through the mail while he drank a glass of water, then finally he opened the bag and removed the burger. He cut it in half carefully, then put it down for us, one piece in each of our bowls.

Meat chomped his half right away, and I was just about to do the same, but I thought about Whiskey. So I bit down on it and trotted out the dog door. Robert didn't say anything, he probably figured I was trying to get my portion away from Meatloaf. That was normal.

I went to the rear yard and stuck my head inside my dog house, then dropped the burger in front of Whiskey. He woke and looked up in surprise, but I left without saying a word and went back in the house.

Robert put the television thing on for a while and we joined him in family room. We sprawled on the floor like dead dogs. I was dyin' to ask Meatloaf what he was about to say about a Pointer, but there wouldn't be a chance until Robert went to bed.

I was curious. I knew that if the information was from Winston, it would be accurate.

Winston was this English Bulldog who was part of our pack, he's very intelligent. His humans are retired school teachers. The male was a college professor, whatever that is. Anyway, they watch a lot of smart television and Winston picks up all these weird facts. He talks different than most dogs.

I think he knows more human words than I do, which is a lot. Most dogs don't bother to learn like I did. All ya gotta do is listen and bury it in your brain.

I have to say that Meatloaf doesn't know many words, unless they're food-related, but he knows a lot of those. I mean, what kinda dog knows what sauté means? So it's not like he's as dumb as they say, he's just got other priorities.

Robert starts flippin' the channels, stopping wherever he sees females with big chests or guns shooting. I don't know a lot about guns, but I know the word and I know what they look like. I know they can kill people, but that's about it. I don't think Robert has a gun.

I went to sleep thinkin' about Whiskey out back. I felt bad for him, because I understand what it's like to be a dog with no food and no home. It's about the saddest thing there is, except for those movies that Robert's girlfriend Shannon likes to watch. I mean, really. Crying over a television picture? What's up with that?

Sometimes I wonder about females. Take Shannon. She acts all feminine, but I get the feeling she's tough underneath. I think if the chips were down, she could hold her own with the males. So why cry at movies?

I'll don't get it, probably never will.

Eventually Robert got up and turned off the television and went upstairs to bed. I watched him climb the stairs, then I heard his big white water dish flush, then I turned to my buddy still asleep on the floor.

"Meat!"

"Uhhhhh."

"Wakeup! Tell me what you were gonna say about Winston and a Pointer."

He opened one eye. "Who's Winston?"

"Meat, come on, wake up. You know who Winston is. What's the story about a Pointer?"

Meatloaf sat up and yawned. "Oh, yeah. Winston. Anyway, he said there was a dog involved in that robbery, and it was…"

"What robbery?" I asked.

"A couple days ago, maybe more, who knows. I was talking to Winston at the park, and we were talking about which dogs were sexier, short hairs or long hairs, and I said I thought short hairs because it's not like mounting a throw rug. My human in Fresno used to have one of those old shag rugs…

"Meat! Focus here. What robbery?"

"The home invasion. You were probably off chasing Simba and didn't hear about it. There was an armed invasion at a house in our neighborhood a bit ago, and the robber had a dog with him."

That didn't make any sense to me. "A dog? Why did he have a dog?"

"I don't know, ask Winston. Anyway, I swear he said it was a white and brown Pointer."

"Wait. Are you sayin' Whiskey was involved in a robbery?"

'I could be wrong, but we got a homeless Pointer in our back yard, so I thought it was a funny coincidence."

It was a funny coincidence. But Whiskey didn't look the criminal dog type, he didn't look mean or angry. He just looked like a friendly mutt. What could a friendly lookin' mutt do in a home invasion robbery?

Still.

I made a memory to talk to Winston the next day at the park. If there was any funny business goin' on, I wanted to know about. Worse, I didn't want to invite a criminal into Robert's home, even if it was just a criminal dog.

Meat didn't make me feel any better with his last comment.

"I told you, dog. I got a bad feeling about this."

THREE
Next Morning, More Questions

I woke up thinkin' the whole idea of Whiskey being a bad dog was all wrong. I knew Winston was prone to stretching the truth or even makin' things up, especially when he talked about himself with female Bulldogs. No dog as nice as Whiskey could be a criminal.

Robert got up early for work. He came down wearin' shiny shoes and a nice coat and some pants that he wouldn't let us rub against. He stood at the counter a while drinkin' his black coffee water and puttin' his thumbs on that little black box he carries around with him. Sometimes he'll talk to it like it was a real person, so I think he must be lonely. He even gave his little box a name. He calls it Black Berry, which is a girl's name, I think.

He likes her better than us, because he gets upset when he can't find her. I get a little jealous when he spends time with that box, I do admit. I mean, he talks to us too, but he seems to like Black Berry better.

Maybe little boxes are a pet you can have when you have thumbs, but dogs don't know about that. Meatloaf says that dogs are born with thumbs, but humans remove them when we're a few days old. It's an old custom, they call it circumcision. Meatloaf says that humans remove our thumbs because if we had them, dogs would rule the world. He thinks it's specism.

Certainly, if I had some, I could open the refrigerator, which is probably why we don't have them. Myself, I think Robert would like it if I could fetch him a beer, but we'll never know.

Robert finished his first meal and went to work, leaving us to entertain ourselves for the day. That can be dangerous, because there's human-bored and there's Labrador-bored. Labrador-bored usually involve digging or chewing something we're not supposed to.

But right now we had Whiskey to deal with, so I thought I'd talk to him for a while. He was awake when I went out to the dog door.

"How you feeling? I asked him. "I wanted to tell you, our master is gone to work, so you can get up and pee if you want."

"Thanks, but I went during the night. It feels good to just to lay here."

I nodded. "Now let me give you a few tips. Did you hear the dog bark next door?"

"Yeah. He sounds mean."

"That's Harley. He's a Rottweiler, but he's a big cupcake, a great dog. I'll tell him you're stayin' here a while."

"Thanks."

I turned around and looked at a bucket on the patio. "Water. We got water in the house, but there's water in that bucket. It catches the rain when it comes." I knew what was next on his list. "You hungry?"

Whiskey nodded.

"Let me see what I can do."

I went back in the house to check the pantry. Robert didn't say anything to us about the missing bread, so we were lucky about that. He probably didn't notice. I nosed around the shelves for something to take.

Lessee…

Pickles, some cans—soup, I think, a jar of peanut butter, napkins—what're those for?—matches, olive oil—yuchh—more cans, applesauce.

Applesauce.

Hmmm. Maybe. There were three of those little plastic cup things with applesauce in them. Robert didn't put those on a higher shelf because Meatloaf refused to eat Robert's fruits or vegetables. Meat

21

says he won't eat them unless he's sure they're organic. I'm not sure what organic fruits and vegetables are, but I think it means they hafta have spots on them. Robert didn't buy those.

I decided on the applesauce. I got one in my mouth and took it out to Whiskey. Meatloaf was in the little room drinkin' from the big white water dish, so I managed to get my stolen food by him unseen.

I dropped the applesauce in the dog house.

"Just chew it all up," I told Whiskey. "I can dig a hole and we can bury the plastic parts you don't eat."

"Thanks, Taser."

Whiskey started to chew while I went inside and got the other two containers and returned to the dog house. I sat down to talk while he ate.

"So, can you tell me anything about where you used to live?" I asked Whiskey.

He stopped licking the spilt applesauce. "I'm not sure where my home is. I came here in a car."

I thought that was interesting.

"You came in a car to this neighborhood?"

"I think so. It was dark when we came."

"Who brought you?"

"My master."

"And then he left you?"

Whiskey hesitated. "I got lost. We got separated. He went one place and I went another."

"You probably weren't hiking in the dark, so maybe you were shopping. Was that it?"

Whiskey looked relieved. "Yeah, that's it. We were shopping at a store, and I had to pee, and my master let me out, and somehow I got lost."

That sounded hard to believe. "He didn't look for you?"

"I'm sure he did. I must have walked too far away. Or something could have happened to him."

"I see."

I didn't want to scare Whiskey off, so I dropped the subject. "How'd you sleep last night?"

"Real good. I just got up once to pee."

"How's the leg?"

"It doesn't bleed anymore, and it feels better. But I can't stand on it."

"Your leg was bleeding?" I hadn't known that before.

"Yeah. But not now. I had a little hole in my coat, like something punctured my skin."

"You gotta watch those cars, buddy."

"Yeah."

I was tired after eating, so I thought a nap would be good. "Whiskey. I'm gonna sleep a little in the sun, just bark if you need anything."

"Thanks, Taser.

He put his head down and I walked over to our little spot of grass for my nap, thinking of our conversation. I couldn't tell if Whiskey was lying or not, but I was anxious to talk to Winston at the park at dusk. I was worried about what I might find out, but I had to know.

***

Just before Robert was due to come home from work, I went out to give Whiskey the lowdown on what to expect during the evening. He was scratchin' his neck with his good back leg. I saw he had a leather collar on but no tag hangin' on it.

"Ok, Whiskey. Now you gotta stay hidden until dark. My master will be home soon, and then we'll eat dinner. Don't worry, I'll bring you some of my chow."

"That would be great. I'm still hungry."

"After we eat, Robert takes us down to the park. Will you be alright here alone?"

"Sure."

23

"How's the leg?"

He sighed. "It still hurts."

"Of course. Rest, take it easy, and don't go in the house for anything." I'm not sure why I said that, it just came out.

"I won't, I'll hide in here." Whiskey cocked his head and looked at me. "I really appreciate you doing this."

"It's not a problem."

"Not for you, but your buddy doesn't seem happy about it."

"Meat doesn't like change, don't worry about him. He takes a while to warm up to new dogs. He'll come around."

I went back in the house to be with Meatloaf. We greeted Robert and then stared at him while he made dinner and ate something that smelled like fish. After that he played with his computer television. I went over and stuck my head under his hand so he'd pet me. That hand didn't seem to be doin' anything important besides changin' channels, so I put it to work.

I think he lost track of time, so we whined until he got up to take us for our nightly walk. He grabbed our leashes from the drawer but didn't hook us up. He just opened the door and let us outside.

I ran ahead to scope things out.

We musta been early, because it was just me and Meatloaf and Gizmo, my Jack Russell buddy. Outside of Meat, Gizmo's my best friend. He was out chasing a ball that his owner was throwin', so I peed on a couple bushes and sniffed out the news from yesterday on the grass.

I smelled all the usual neighborhood dogs, but when I wandered over to the far end of the park, I got a hit of somethin' really weird. I had my sniffer stuck on it when Meatloaf saw me and ran over to check it out himself.

We kept our nose on the same spot, until finally Meatloaf looked up.

"What is that, Taser?"

I stopped sniffin'. "Dunno. Smells like a cat, doesn't it?"

He shook his head. "No cat I ever smelled."

We were still checkin' it out when Gizmo ran up and joined us.

"Hey guys, whatcha find?"

"We're not sure."

Gizmo put his nose on it, too. He jerked back after one whiff. "Wow. Smells wild, doesn't it? That ain't no alley cat. Ain't no coyote, either."

WOOF WOOF!

We turned around at the bark and saw it was Winston arriving at the park. His master let him off the leash and then walked over to join the other humans talking in a group. His master has this big belly and always has a cigar in his mouth. It stinks bad, which is probably why he does it outside on the walk.

"I gotta talk to Winston," I said, and ran over to him. Finally, I thought, we could get some information on the robbery.

Winston is the neighborhood know-it-all because his retired master walks him twice a day all around our streets. He knows dogs I'd never met.

I barked at the squat Bulldog. "Hi Winston."

"G'day, my friend." He looked over as Meatloaf and Gizmo joined us. He nodded at them. "Mornin' lads. What's the bother over there?"

"Some strange animal scent," Gizmo said. "We're not sure what it is."

"I'm not surprised," Winston said. "Any manner of wild animal can simply walk in here from upper Arizona. There are reliable reports of mountain lions not far from here."

Meatloaf looked concerned. "Do mountain lions eat Labradors?"

Gizmo nudged me. "Yeah. But only Chocolate Labradors."

Winston shook his head. "It's bad enough we have to deal with these blasted coyotes, now we have new predators trying to eat us."

"What new predator?" asked a familiar soft voice. "Do I have to worry about something new?"

25

I turned and saw it was Simba, a Golden Retriever and my favorite female. I tried to put her at ease. "We're still investigating, Simba, don't be worried yet."

"Yeah," said Gizmo. "You can worry after one of us dogs gets eaten. I don't like how these things can jump our fence."

"It's specism, said Meatloaf. "Humans put us outside to get eaten while they hide in their house."

"Hey, those dog doors go both ways. A mountain lion could come in the house, too."

Simba shivered.

I changed the subject before the group got too carried away. "Hey Winston, what can you tell me about that neighborhood robbery? Meatloaf said you mentioned it a while back. Something about a robbery with a dog involved."

Winston sat on his haunches. "Yes, yes. You mean the home invasion. Quite the mess, I must say. I'm surprised your friend didn't tell you."

"I forgot," Meatloaf admitted.

Winston nodded, knowingly. "Well. It was an armed robbery occurring sometime after dinner time. There was knock at the door and the resident looked out the window and saw a man standing there with a pathetic canine on a leash. The situation didn't seem out of sorts so he opened the door. A weapon appeared and a bloke came in threatening to shoot."

"You mean the robber used the dog to get inside?" I asked.

"Quite so. It was a sad looking creature, the home owner assumed the man had found a lost dog and was trying to assist him."

Gizmo snorted. "That's awful."

Winston agreed. "A despicable ruse, at best. Anyway, the blaggard got away with some valuable jewelry."

"How'd they get away? In a car?"

Winston thought. "As I remember, they went off on foot. I suppose there could have been an accomplice waiting who drove them off."

"What ever happened to the dog?" I asked.

Winston shrugged. "I don't believe anyone knows."

"We know where he is," Meatloaf blurted out before I could stop him.

"Meat! We don't know that, yet." I turned back to Winston. "Do you know what kind of dog it was?"

"Yes, a Pointer, I believe. A German Short Hair. Why do you ask? Do you know something?" He looked at Meatloaf.

Luckily Meatloaf didn't answer, because we saw Remi, the obnoxious poodle show up and walk over to our group.

Gizmo nodded politely at him. "Hey, Remi."

Everyone else ignored him. We always got the feeling Remi considered himself better than the rest of us dogs, so we treated him like we would a cat living under the same roof—with suspicion and distrust.

The sun was down and it was turning dark, so I wanted to get all the information I could gather before we had to leave.

"This dog," I asked. "Do you know what color he was?"

Winston stared up at the darkening sky like he was looking for the answer. "Well. I believe he was white and tan. Or was it brown?" He scratched behind one ear. "It might have been gray and tan. Something like that."

Remi butted in. "Are you talking about the Canine Caper? The home invasion in our neighborhood? It was all over the news, you dumb mutts. You do follow the news, don't you?"

Meatloaf leaned over. "Hey Remi. Go bite yourself Or I will."

Remi didn't look concerned. He blinked his weeping eyes. "My, my. Threats of bodily harm from the 'Meatloaf' creature. I'm positively terrified."

Meat growled. "Shut your yap, pencil pinkie."

"Hey, guys." I held up a paw. "Save it for later." I tried to get the last bit of information I needed from Winston. "So who was it?"

Winston cocked his head. "Who was the robber?"

27

"No, who got robbed, which house? It was someone in our neighborhood, right?"

Winston backed up two steps. "Yes, well, I can't really say. Sorry."

This wasn't normal for the talkative Bulldog. "You can't tell us whose house got robbed?" I asked.

"I must go now." Winston turned and ran back to his master.

I looked at my friends. "That was weird."

"What was weird?" a new arrival asked.

It was Roxie, the Fox Terrier. She was one of our pack, a great girl with lots of moxie. She doesn't take any lip from the guys.

"The Canine Caper," said Remi. "Do you know whose house was robbed?"

"No," Roxie said. "But I thought Winston knew all about it."

"He's covering something up," I said. "Winston knows who it is."

Remi sniffed. "Is this another of your boring little mysteries, Taser? Another occasion for you to stick your nose in human business? Really."

Gizmo stuck up for me. "Hey! Taser is the one dog we can count on to watch our neighborhood."

"To that I must say, who asked him? The meddling mutt just brings trouble for our breed."

Remi talked like I wasn't even there.

"If you're worried about trouble," I said. "You better worry about what new predator left its scent over at the far end of the park."

Remi turned his head around with a jerk. "Where! What is it?"

"We're not sure," I said. "It's some kind of animal we haven't smelled around here before. Probably came down out of the mountains lookin' for fresh meat."

"Yeah," said Meatloaf. "Fresh Poodle meat."

I got on my feet. "Roxie, you've got an experienced nose, let's go see what you think."

We left the pack and ran over to the other side of the park at a fast clip, then I showed her the spot. She sniffed it once, then again. She looked up me. "I know what this is. I used to live further north, up close to the forest."

"Is it bad news?"

She nodded. "Especially for us dogs. One of these took a Cocker Spaniel, my best friend in Payson. There were pieces of her all over the back yard."

"Wow. I'm sorry, Roxie."

"We're gonna have to be on our toes now. You know what Winston used to say when he talked about approaching danger?"

I knew the phrase, it had stuck in my mind ever since he said it.

Something wicked this way comes.

***

It was finally dark when the creature emerged from the sandwash behind the row of human houses. It had been waiting for the cover of the night, ignoring his hunger pains until it was time to hunt. It did not hide because it was afraid, it hid for advantage, because this vicious animal feared very little, not even man.

He emerged from cover because it was time to eat.

The creature looked left and right, then followed his nose directly over to a two-story home bordering the wide-open desert. It crouched down as it came closer, convinced it couldn't be seen in the near darkness. The patient hunter flexed his claws as it anticipated finding prey.

The smell it picked up was not only of dog, it was of wounded dog, the same smell he'd found under the weeping Mesquite tree near the highway. A wounded animal would be an easy meal, unlike the jittery rabbits he normally pursued, skinny rabbits picked-over by his coyote competition.

While both carnivores would eat the same prey, the coyotes stayed away from this creature. Coyotes knew their kind was no match for

29

the speed and aggression of forty pounds of fury, should this clawed beast choose to attack them.

It crouched on the desert floor behind some scrawny brush and stared through the fence at the doghouse in the backyard. His next victim laid sleeping or resting inside the doghouse, unaware of the advancing threat. Satisfied with conditions, the creature leapt to the top of the block fence post and balanced there, looking down on his waiting meal, assessing the best attack.

He was just about to jump in the backyard when he heard the approaching noise of two panting dogs out front, followed closely by a male human.

The bobcat hissed but retreated from his perch on the fence post and walked slowly back out in the desert. Tonight he would have to satisfy himself with a skinny rabbit. He would return another time for this wounded prey.

Soon.

FOUR
Later that night.

Meatloaf and I joined Robert in the television room. He would stop flippin' channels whenever a female chest appeared, watch it a while and then flip again to find another chest. I don't know why. Maybe they weren't big enough. Meatloaf says Robert is looking for one special chest and he can't find it, so he keeps looking.

You would think one female chest would be as good as another, but I guess not.

It was distracting. After a while I wanted to think clearly, so I went in the living room.

I don't know why Robert calls it the living room, because we do all our living in the television room, which is what he calls the family room, which is weird because he doesn't have a family. It's just him. I guess Robert thinks me and Meatloaf are his family.

Cool.

No matter, the living room is good for thinking. So I lay down in there on the rug by myself and tried to analyze what Winston told us at the park. It was weird he wouldn't tell us who got robbed. I suppose something about that detail was important to the crime. The problem was, I wanted to make sure the dog used in the robbery wasn't Whiskey, and I didn't know where to investigate.

Winston wasn't sure of the dog's color, but he said it was a Pointer, and that was serious enough. Still, I didn't believe Whiskey was a bad dog. Dogs are loyal to their master, no matter if the master is a criminal or not. The problem was, if the bad master came lookin' for Whiskey, I was inviting trouble for Robert.

31

My job was to protect my master's home, not to bring danger to it. I thought I needed to get more information out of Whiskey. He was my best source now.

I got up and went outside quietly. I had brought Whiskey a couple mouthfuls of my dog food dinner earlier, along with a cup of dry noodles stolen from the pantry. What I needed to get him was a big meal, something like the Thanksgiving turkey leftovers we had a while ago. But how I might find a meal like that would take more thinking. Right now I had to confront Whiskey.

He looked up when I walked over.

"Is anything wrong?" he asked. "Do I have to leave?"

"No, everything's fine," I said.

I sat down at the doghouse door. It was getting colder outside. I thought Whiskey must be happy to have someplace to keep warm at night. "I just came out to talk. Meatloaf and Robert are inside watchin' the television box."

"What's a television box?"

"You know, that picture thing with all the female chests and loud explosions."

"Oh, that."

I thought a direct approach might be best. "Say, Whiskey. I want you to know we're friends, Ok? I'm gonna help you, no matter what."

"Sure, Taser. I know."

"But here's the problem. I found out about that robbery in our neighborhood, the one with a dog."

Whiskey looked down at his paws but didn't say anything.

"I got an idea you might have been involved with it. Somebody said it was a Pointer that the robber brought to the front door to get in. The people looked out and saw this guy with a pathetic looking dog and opened the door."

Whiskey still wouldn't speak.

"Come on. What can you tell me about it?" I said. "I've got to know."

He took a big breath and let it out slowly. "I'm not gonna lie to you Taser, you're the only on who has ever helped me."

I could hardly believe my big ears. "It was you? You were at the home robbery?"

Whiskey nodded. "But I tell you, I didn't know that's what my master was going to do. See, he rescued me from the dog pound, I wasn't with him very long, I didn't know he was a robber."

"How long did he have you?"

"I'm not sure. I can't count. But it was after the hot time."

"How many big moons did you see?"

"What's a moon?"

I thought to myself that Whiskey should have paid more attention to human words, but I know most dogs are like that. "Moon. The night-light. How many times did the night-light get big?"

"Ahh. Just once."

"So you were only with him a short time. Like maybe he came to the pound to get a sad-looking dog to use in the robbery."

Whiskey spoke loudly. "No! It's not like that, he loves me."

"I'm sure he does, but maybe it didn't start out like that."

"He gives me food and water!"

"Ok, that's good." I didn't want to upset him any more. "So where is your master now? Tell me what happened that night."

"I'm sorry, Taser. I shouldn't talk about it."

"Whiskey, please. I'm your friend. Tell me."

He put on a face like he'd been caught peeing on the carpet. I felt sorry for the poor pooch.

He sighed again. "We came out here in his car. My master parked on the side of the road and we got out and went for a walk. I thought it was so I could poop, because I had to go, so I went on somebody's grassy yard. But then we went up to the door of another house."

He looked at me like he was uncomfortable with his confession, so I encouraged him to keep talkin'.

"Yeah, Ok. Then what happened?"

"I heard a mean dog bark inside the house, so I got a little scared. He didn't sound friendly."

A dog. That was interesting. That meant it was a dog owner who got robbed, and Winston knew all the dogs in the neighborhood. I knew most of them myself. Winston was holding back valuable information for some reason. I wondered if the mutt was one I knew.

"Ok," I said. "Go on."

"So the man in the house..."

I stopped him talking so I wouldn't forget to ask. "What did the man in the house look like?"

"He was old, but he still had some muscles on his arms. He had those drawings on his arms, too."

"Drawings. Yeah, I know what you mean. Ok."

"So the old human looks out the side window and he sees us, and then my master waves all friendly-like, so the old guy opens the door. And then my master pushes him backwards and goes inside. I didn't, though."

"Didn't what?"

"I didn't go inside the house, because this mean dog was barking and I was afraid. I ran out to the street and sat down and waited. I heard arguing and fighting, and pretty soon my master came out and we ran away down the street. That's when it happened."

"What? What happened?"

"I heard this real loud noise, and then another, and that's when we got hurt."

"Hurt?"

"Yes, my leg hurt real bad, and my master got hurt in his arm. He had blood on him and everything. I thought it was from the dog bites."

"Bites? From the dog in the house?"

"Yeah, the mean dog bit my master."

"Ok. Let's talk about the loud noise, what did it sound like?"

34

"It sounded like your television." He looked over at the house. "Like that noise right now."

Robert was watching some police show on the television. Guns. I should have known.

"Whiskey, did you really get hit by a car on that leg?"

"No. I'm sorry, that was not true. I got hurt right then with my master."

I knew that was it, but I wanted to see if he'd tell the truth. I wanted to see if he really was a good dog. "Whiskey, I think you were shot getting away. Whoever your master robbed came out and shot at him with a gun. It sounds like you and your master were hit."

He shook his muzzle slowly. "I can't believe a nice old man like that would own a gun, much less shoot at us."

I stared down my snout like I was talkin' to a puppy. "Whiskey, come on. This is Arizona. Everyone has a gun."

I thought a minute, then I said, "Come out of that dog house and let me get a good look at that leg."

Whiskey hobbled out cautiously and stood on the patio, his bad leg tucked up close to his body. The window door shades were closed, so Robert wouldn't be able to see us standing there.

"Now turn around so the window light shines on it."

He turned around and I looked closely at his bad rear leg. I saw a weird mark on his left haunch; it looked like a little hole. I kept looking. Finally I saw another little hole behind it.

"It looks like the gun bullet went right through your skin. That's why you're not sicker."

"It still hurts."

"It's a gun bullet wound," I said. "Gun bullets can kill you. You're a lucky dog, my friend."

"I've been licking the sore spots."

"Good. It seems to be helping, so keep it up. Now, let's try to figure this out. What happened after you got shot?"

Whiskey looked around the backyard, and then at the house. "Can I go back in my dog house now?"

He seemed a little skittish, for good reason. I'd forgotten about Robert for a minute. "Sorry, yeah. Good idea, stay out of sight."

He hobbled back in the little house and lay down, then told me. "I think after the robbery we went back to the car. That's when my master gave me this pouch and we got separated."

My head jerked up. "Whoa! Wait a minute. What pouch?"

"The little pouch hanging from my collar," Whiskey said. "I think it's made of leather."

This confused me. "I don't see a pouch."

He raised his chin so I could get a better look. "It's right here."

I looked again closely at his collar, but I didn't see anything on it, not even a tag. "Whiskey. I don't know how to tell you this, but there's no pouch hangin' from your collar. Nothin'."

Suddenly he looked worried. "Are you sure? My master said it was very valuable."

"Dog. Trust me, there's nothin' there but your collar. You must have lost it." When I told him that, he started whining like Meatloaf does when dinner comes late.

Hennnngggg. Hennnngggg. Hennnngggg.

"Maybe it's in the yard," I said.

"No! I would have seen it." Whiskey barked louder. "Was it on my collar when you met me in the park that night?"

"I don't think so. You must have lost it when you were wanderin' around out in the desert."

Hennnngggg. Hennnngggg. Hennnngggg.

"Whiskey, don't be upset, we'll think of somethin'." Then I thought. "What was in the pouch?"

He put his head on his front paws and sighed, then looked up. "I don't know, but it was important."

Maybe the robber tied it on Whiskey's collar and sent him away so the police wouldn't get it. He didn't sound like he cared as much about

36

Whiskey as he did about money. That didn't seem like a good master to me.

"How'd you get separated?" I asked.

"It's my fault. We stopped at a store and my master went inside. He said something about bandages."

I cocked my head. "He went in a store to get a bandage? For your gun bullet wound?"

"I guess. It's my fault. He was gone so long I got scared and I went out the window and went to look for him. Then I got lost."

"Where was the store?"

"I'm trying to think." Whiskey was quiet a minute. "I can't remember. I think it was close by. Do you suppose we could look for it?"

I didn't think that would be a good idea. I definitely didn't want to run into this robber criminal in case he was lookin' for Whiskey.

"We'll see. I better get back inside. We can talk about it tomorrow."

FIVE
Next morning, trouble

BANG BANG BANG.

It's never a good sign when the neighbors come over and beat on your door instead of using the door bell.

BANG BANG BANG.

We can be loud, too.

WOOF! WOOF! BOW! WOW! WOOF! WOOF!

After Meatloaf and I warned the visitor, I took a look out the door-side window to see who it was.

Oh-oh.

"Who is it Taser?"

"It's Mister Crenshaw. He looks mad."

Meatloaf yawned. "He's head of the Homeowners Association. Those guys are always mad."

I wondered what we could have done to warrant a visit, then I figured he might have seen me out of the yard when I first met Whiskey at the park. They got all these official neighborhood rules about keeping dogs on leashes and about cleaning up your dog's poop. Taking away dog poop? How rude is that? We need that poop right where it falls so we can sniff it and find out what's up around here.

Robert left his breakfast and came to the front door. He opened it up and talked to mister Crenshaw for a while. Actually, mister Crenshaw did most of the talking. Robert just stood there like he was thinking about baseball, or female chests, or somethin'. But he was polite. Which is more than I would have been.

Anyway, I listened and heard some of the words.

38

Night…sneaky   dog…talked   …before…warning…garage…last time…steak…rules…big fine.

I cocked my head and tried to figure out what Crenshaw was mad about, but it didn't make sense to me.

"What's he saying?" Meatloaf asked.

"I think he's blaming me for somethin' I didn't do."

Ever since I chased his precious cat around his open garage, old man Crenshaw thinks I'm a bad dog. Maybe he shouldn't have left his garage door open. What's he think, I'm not gonna investigate an open garage? That's where people keep their dog food. How did I know his stupid cat was in there? That was when he first moved in, but he's never forgiven me.

Oh, and there's that barkin' all-night-long issue that time Robert went out of town.

And there's that time Meatloaf took a huge dump on his driveway.

And there's the time I was diggin' in his flower…

"Taser! What's he saying," Meatloaf demanded.

"Something about a sneaky dog, for one."

"He must be talking about you."

"And something about a big fine and a steak and his garage."

"Oh that."

I looked right into my buddy's eyes. "Oh what?"

Just then Robert said goodbye to Mister Crenshaw and looked down where we were hangin' our heads. He shook his finger at us but didn't say nothin' about being bad dogs. I guess he suspected somethin' but couldn't prove it. Either that or he thinks all these neighborhood rules are goofy.

He left us by the front door and went back in the other room to finish his breakfast. Normally, we'd be in there watchin' him eat, waitin' for a stray piece of bacon to fall on the floor, but I wanted to talk to Meatloaf.

"What do you mean, oh that?" I asked him.

39

Meatloaf looked down at the floor. "You know when I was late getting to the park last night?"

"Yeah."

"Well, Robert was ahead of me talking to someone, and I got a faint whiff of red meat from Crenshaw's garage. So I had to check it out."

I shook my head, I should have known it would involve food. "And then what happened?"

"Old man Crenshaw was thawing a couple frozen steaks in his garage. He shouldn't get mad, I only took one."

"You stole a frozen steak?"

"Actually, it was mostly thawed."

"That was a bad idea, Meatloaf.

"Don't be so critical. I have traumatic survival syndrome."

"What's that?"

"Fear of hunger."

I sighed. "Did you eat all of the steak?"

"I didn't have time to eat any," he said. "I left it under his front bush. The big bush next to his garage."

"What the heck for?"

"Had to. I couldn't take it with me to the park. So I figured you'd sneak out today and get it. I figured it would be good for Whiskey."

That's what I mean about my buddy, he always surprises you. "Look, that's great for Whiskey, but Crenshaw! That's like stealing from the dogcatcher. He could make real trouble for us."

"Big deal. Crenshaw doesn't scare me."

When you get a little older, like Meatloaf, and you been around the block a few times, this human yellin' stuff just rolls off your back.

"Ok," I said. "I'll get the steak after everyone has gone to work on our street. Right now I gotta tell Harley what's up."

I ran out the dog door and over to Harley's side of the yard. I could hear the big Rottweiler lappin' water out of his bowl on the patio, so I called out.

WOOF WOOF

40

He met me back in the yard corner. We couldn't see each other, but we could hear each other better through the view fence.

Harley's voice was deep. "Wassup, dog?"

"Hey Harley, just a little heads up. I got a friend stayin' with me a while, I thought I'd explain why."

"Yeah, I smells the pooch over there. He friendly?"

"Very friendly. Problem is, he's homeless right now, and his back leg got hurt. I'm tryin' to hide him here from Robert until his leg gets well."

"What's the dog's problem?"

I wasn't sure if I should tell him, but I knew it was gonna come out soon among the neighborhood dogs. "He was involved in a shooting and he got hit by a gun bullet."

Harley snorted. "Dog's a criminal? You harborin' fugitives over there now, Jack?"

"No, no, Whiskey's not a fugitive. Well, he's kind of a fugitive, he's hiding from his master. His master is the criminal."

"Lemme tell you Jack, that's not what it be like. When you a dog and you gots a criminal master, that makes you a criminal, too. It's somethin' about aidin' and abettin' the situation. You a smart dog, you oughta know that."

"Harley, that's not how it is."

"Sheet, Jack. That's how it is in my old neighborhood. If the po-leece man hadn't arrested us and found me a home here, I'd be a criminal still, just like my old master."

I sighed. I could see I wasn't gonna get anywhere with Harley. "Just keep it to yourself, Ok?"

"That's cool. I ain't no squealer dog."

I left Harley and went to the front gate, thinkin' the neighbors should be off to work by now and I could get the stolen steak. I stopped at the dog house and told Whiskey I was on to somethin', and then I flipped the gate latch with my nose.

I was lucky. Sometimes Robert puts a lock on it, but he takes it off when he takes out the garbage can and he forgets to put it back on.

Anyway, in a minute I was out.

Old man Crenshaw's place was only two houses away. Unfortunately it was right on our way to the park. I crept along the bushes in front of the house next door to me, pausing to check out Crenshaw's place next door.

Cat Crap.

Crenshaw's garage door was open. The old guy didn't work at a job anymore, he just went around the neighborhood, yellin' at people for forgettin' to take their garbage cans off the street, or to pull their weeds, or how they had to keep their dogs on a leash.

What's up with that? A leash? Mister Crenshaw didn't keep his cat on a leash. Meatloaf would call that specism.

So I didn't know what to do. The steak was under a bush right next to his garage door. I didn't want to go home and wait, I figured some other dog or maybe even a coyote would get to it before I got back.

So I'm down low, creepin' on my belly like one of those war dogs in Afghanhoundland I see on television news, and I'm close enough to smell the steak, and all of a sudden Crenshaw's fat Burmese cat walks out of the garage.

I freeze.

The stupid cat takes a couple more steps, but all of a sudden it turns its creepy head and looks right in my eyes. I didn't know what to do, because I was afraid Crenshaw was right there inside the garage. But I had to chance it. I got up and ran under the bush and bit into the steak, but suddenly the cat arches his back and starts with this disgusting awful hissing-yowl thing, and then old man Crenshaw comes out and sees me with the steak, which means I'm caught red-pawed right there. He yells at me like I'm some sort of sneaky low-down egg-sucking dog.

HEY!

That was it. I turn around and run like Lassie on fire all the way back to my gate. The steak meat was half-hangin' outta my mouth, floppin' around like crazy as I ran, but I make it back home and through my gate alright. I take the hunk of red meat right back to Whiskey and drop it in his doghouse doorway.

He was too shocked to speak.

Then I ran in the house and lay down in the hallway like everythin' was all nice and normal. But then…

BANG BANG BANG.

Meatloaf was sprawled out in his usual position in the hall, which is on his flat side, legs straight out. He raised his head and looked at me. "Isn't that old man Crenshaw's knock?" he asked.

BANG BANG BANG.

"Maybe. Better stay away from the door," I told him.

Meatloaf put his head back down. "Right. Can't be too-cautious. You never know what kind of creepy human might be out there.

***

It was an older American car, something not often seen in the expensive North Scottsdale neighborhood. The faded and dented Chevrolet Malibu cruised slowly up and down the well-kept streets, pausing now and then as the driver peered into house yards. It looked like he was searching for a delivery address or a home that needed some landscape work. Older cars or work trucks cruising for job leads were a common sight, and no resident who might have seen this particular car would take notice.

The car pulled over to the side of the street and driver got out with a hand-scrawled paper sign and a roll of silver duct tape. He taped the piece of paper to a metal stop-sign post at the end of one of the streets leading out of the subdivision. Then he stepped back to admire his work. Yes, he thought, everyone will see that. Satisfied, he returned to his car and his drive around the neighborhood.

The driver slumped slightly, driving with a dirty baseball cap pulled low over his eyes, one hand on the steering wheel and one hand on the paper bag on the seat with a 9mm pistol inside. The pistol was a messy but necessary precaution, a last resort tool.

He didn't want to shoot the Pointer, he'd grown attached to the damn thing during the brief time he'd had it, but money was money and dogs were, well, just dogs. There would always be another sad-faced pooch. There would not, however, be another dog carrying around a little pouch with nearly a million dollars in it.

So if he had to shoot the dog should it try to run away from him, so be it. He could buy another dog. He could buy a kennel of dogs, if he wanted. But at the moment all he wanted was a limping brown and white mutt he'd named after his favorite drink.

He knew it was risky hiding the jewelry bag on Whiskey's collar after the robbery, but it was better he take that risk than get caught with stolen goods and get sent back to the slammer. Besides, at the time he didn't know how valuable the coin might be.

He moved his sore arm up and down gingerly to test its function. The homeowner's bullet had only grazed his shoulder, so after applying a pint of disinfectant and ingesting a pint of whiskey, he felt just fine. He was glad the bullet wound wasn't on his shooting arm. He may need it yet.

The dented Chevy Malibu drove down Taser and Meatloaf's little street and cruised right by a two-story house where an irate old man banged on the front door.

The driver ignored the old man but noticed the neighborhood park a few houses ahead. He stopped his vehicle in the shade of a huge Palo Verde tree overhanging the street, then got out with another piece of paper. He taped it sloppily to the face of a metal sign at the entrance to the park.

His task done in the area, he returned to his car and drove to the next subdivision across the highway to leave more of his notices. Somewhere, he knew, a soft-hearted homeowner was caring for an injured brown and white short-haired Pointer. Sooner or later the fool would see one of the lost-dog signs and call with a home address and an invitation to come get the sad creature.

SIX
That Same Evening

I got a little nervous on our way to the park. I thought maybe Mister Crenshaw would be outside his house and yell at us, but we ran right by without a problem.

Most of the pack was already there, even Harley with Doctor Bill's new wife. Harley never got to go to the park with us before the new female took him, which everyone thinks is cool, especially Roxie. But I didn't see the one dog I wanted to talk to—Winston. I couldn't help wonderin' if he was hiding from me and my questions.

I sniffed all over to see if I could pick up Winston's scent, but all I got was older smells. No problem. I figured he might show up yet.

Some of the humans were standing around the park sign and staring at it. I went over to see what was up. Then I saw a piece of white paper taped on the sign.

"What's up, Taser?"

I turned. It was Simba, my best girl. We were kinda mates, but we lived in separate houses. Everyone knew we were close.

"Hi beautiful," I said. Simba had this great golden coat, it was always soft and shiny. I bumped into her playfully and she bumped me back, but at the moment I was too focused on Whiskey and his problem to think about mounting.

Which means I was really focused.

"Watcha lookin' at," she asked me.

"That sign." I pointed with my nose. "I wish I could read." I looked closer, and then I noticed it had a picture of a dog on it. "Is somebody selling a dog?"

46

"I'll check." Simba walked over closer and stood with the humans. One of them reached down and patted her head, and her tail switched back and forth in appreciation. She stood there a while and then ran back over.

"I heard our masters talking, and it looks like somebody lost a dog," she said. "The picture looks like a Pointer."

Uh-oh.

This was bad news. This was very bad news.

I wanted to keep Whiskey a secret, so I ran over to the group to talk with them, hoping to change the subject. Simba followed me over and stood next to me.

"Hey guys," I said. "What's up?"

Gizmo was talking. "We're telling Harley about the robbery. You know, that home invasion."

Harley stuck out his chest and spoke in his deep voice. "Tell you what, Jack. Ain't nobody invadin' my house. I be protectin' my master with these."

He bared his vicious-looking Rottweiler teeth.

"Oh my," said Roxie.

Roxie's got this thing for Harley.

Simba said sadly, "I can't do much protecting, but my master doesn't have much money or nice things to worry about."

"What about your television?"

"Everyone has a television."

"Do they have a computer? Or any jewelry?"

"Jewelry?" Meatloaf asked. "Who wants jewelry?"

"Everybody," said Simba. "Every female, anyway."

"Is that what they took in the home invasion robbery?"

"Winston said it was jewelry, or something valuable like that."

"One thing I don't understand," said Gizmo, "is this whole jewelry thing. Why do female humans hang shiny stones on their bodies? What's the point?"

"The stones are pretty," said Simba. "It makes the females happy."

47

I thought I knew better. "Nope. Females put sparkly things on their neck to blind the males, so they won't notice the female has a small chest."

Harley disagreed. "No, Jack, that ain't it. It's just bling. It's just for fun."

"It's more than that," said Roxie. "It's a symbol. See, when the male human gets in trouble for sniffing other female humans, his mate makes him spend ridiculous amounts of money for little shiny stones. Then the female wears these shiny stones on her body when they go out, to show everyone what a chump her mate is."

"What makes these stones so valuable?"

Simba knew. "There are only a hundred shiny stones in the whole world. They dug them out of the ground years ago in the country of New York. Everyone wants them now, so they cost a lot to buy."

Meatloaf shook his head. "I don't understand the big deal. If I can't eat it or mount it, I got no use for it."

"Where do they buy these shiny stones?"

"Craigslist."

"That's not true," Simba said. "You have to go to a special jewelry-selling store where clerks make the male human feel guilty if he doesn't spend a lot of money."

WOOF WOOF.

We turned around and saw it was Winston waddling up to the park, pulling hard on the leash of his male master.

Winston ran over, pantin' furiously with his pink tongue hangin' out. "Huh Huh Huh. Hello lads, ladies" he said. "Sorry I'm late. Master went out for burgers and chips. What's new?"

"We're talkin' about the robbery."

"Yes, yes. The robbery. Bad business."

"What more can you tell us?"

"Uhh. Uh, let's see." Winston seemed at a loss for words, and then he changed the subject. "Have you seen all the lost dog posters? They're up all over our neighborhood. Poor thing."

"Did you say lost dog?" Harley asked.

I knew it was gonna be too hard to keep my secret any longer, so I thought I'd better confess the truth. Besides, I needed their help. "Look, guys, I gotta tell you somethin'. A couple nights ago, this stray dog came to our backyard lookin like death. I had to help it, so I let him in the yard. He's stayin' in my dog house right now, hiding from Robert."

Simba looked at me suspiciously. "Is this a female dog you're keeping?"

Oh brother.

"No, it's a male. His name is Whiskey."

Then Harley the Rottweiler blurted it out. "Poor dog's been shot. Taser's nursin' him back to health."

"Gunshot!" asked Winston. "Is this a Pointer, per chance?"

I couldn't lie. "Yes, Winston, this is the same dog used in the robbery."

"No!"

"You're hiding a criminal?" Roxie asked.

I protested. "He's a victim, not a criminal. His master used him to get in the house so he could rob the homeowner. He's a good dog, really. He didn't know what was happening."

The dogs looked at each other, and then Roxie said: "What can we do to help?"

It seemed they finally saw the value in helping. "I need food for him, he's weak. Anything you can get me would be great."

"Right," said Winston. "But are you sure he's a good bloke?"

"I'm sure."

OK, I wasn't sure.

Winston looked uncomfortable as he stammered. "Uh...this dog, your Pointer friend. I must tell you, this is a serious development. It's a matter of utmost importance we find his master. He's taken something that must not be discovered by authorities or given to the underworld."

49

I cocked my head and asked. "Does this have to do with who got robbed? Somethin' you won't talk about?"

Winston nodded. "I'm terribly sorry, I'm sworn to secrecy on that matter. Trust me when I tell you, an article of extreme importance was taken. A human life depends on its safe return. I must speak to this stray as soon as possible to find out what he knows."

"Are you talkin' about the little leather bag they stole?" I asked.

Winston jumped up and down, his jowls floppin' in the air. "Yes! Do you have it? It must be returned immediately!"

"Leather bag? What leather bag?" Meatloaf asked.

"A jewelry bag," I said. "Look, Winston. That's the problem. You see, Whiskey did have the little leather bag…"

"I thought you said he was a good dog." Simba said.

"He is a good dog," I protested. "The robber tied the stolen bag to Whiskey's collar and then set him free. I think he was gonna get the bag later after things cooled down, but they got separated while Whiskey was recuperating, and then—"

"Wait a minute. This whole thing sounds fishy to me," said Gizmo. "How do you know this isn't part of their plan? Maybe the robber is waiting for someone who's got Whiskey to call? Then he'll take the dog and the jewelry."

"Whiskey doesn't have the jewelry now, I tell you."

"Maybe he knows where it is."

I didn't think so. "He said he lost it somewhere."

Harley the Rottweiler spoke up. "Maybe they runnin' a game on you, Jack. You sure 'bout this dog?"

I didn't say anything, because I couldn't be sure, I only had my instincts.

"Taser," Winston said. "We have to assume you are correct. I propose we get this dog some food to keep his strength up. Then, we need a proper search for the lost leather bag. Can Whiskey accompany you?"

"No, his back leg is still in bad shape. It hurts too much to walk far."

50

"Right. Then speak with him to determine his previous locations."

"Good plan." I knew it was a long shot, but it was our only chance. I told the pack. "We'll have to backtrack his route through the desert. I can go first thing tomorrow morning, who can come with me?"

"I'll go," said Gizmo.

"I can come, if Gizmo will open my gate," said Roxie.

Gizmo nodded. "No problem."

That was three of us. Three was a good group size, any more would attract attention. That reminded me we were at the park for exercise. I looked over at our humans.

"Ok," I said. "Now, we better go chase the ball for your master, Gizmo, so we keep him happy. Otherwise, our humans are gonna get suspicious."

SEVEN
Next Morning, a Desert Explore

I woke early and snuck out the dog door to talk to Whiskey, because I was feelin' the pressure to solve our problem. I knew we were runnin' out of time. I was afraid Robert would find our hidden friend on one of his poop pickup days, so I had to get the information we needed to find that lost bag.

I still didn't understand how a little leather pouch could be so important, no matter how much money or what kind of jewelry was in it. Winston said it was a matter of life and death. I knew that money could be important, but I didn't think it was that serious. Robert said money was only important if you didn't have any.

Maybe jewelry was a matter of life and death, certainly Simba seemed to think so. That's probably why Meatloaf says golden-hair dogs are high maintenance.

Whiskey was awake when I walked up.

"Hey Whiskey, how's the leg?"

He stood up. "Better. I can stand on it without much pain, but walking is still painful."

"Good. Now, here's the plan. I got some friends coming over to help me look for your pouch."

His face lit up like Meatloaf at mealtime. It was the first time I'd seen him happy.

"Taser, that would be great, but I don't think I can be much help." He looked at his back leg. "It's my wound."

"Don't worry, we can look for it. But you gotta tell me where to look, the path you took to get here. How much do you remember after the robbery?"

"To tell you the truth, my brain got confused after I got hit with the gun bullet. I was thinking about my hurt leg. I didn't pay enough attention to where I was."

"Of course." I tried to help him. "Do you remember if that store was close by to us?"

"I think so. If only I hadn't gone to look for my master, I wouldn't have lost him."

Whiskey head drooped after he said that.

I kept talkin' so he wouldn't be sad. "Ok, so you were in our house subdivision. Then you went to the robbery, then the store, then you went to find your master. What happened after that?"

"I walked a long way until my leg hurt real bad, then I stopped and lay down under a tree. I tried to sleep."

That was interesting. "Where was this tree?"

"It was close to the highway. I remember loud cars and trucks waking me up." He pointed across the desert in the direction of the big road. "Off that way."

"Good. Do you remember what kind of tree it was?" I pointed at one out in the back. "Was it like that?"

He stuck his head out of the dog house and looked. "Yeah, like that one. A real big tree."

A Mesquite tree.

I made a memory, but wasn't sure it would help to know what kind, because there was a million of them out there.

I thanked Whiskey and went back inside, 'cause it was almost time for Robert to come down for breakfast. If he didn't see me waitin' for him he'd know I was up to somethin'.

Meatloaf sat by the foot of the stairs. We usually wait near the bottom step and whine every now and then when Robert doesn't come down fast enough.

We hear the same thing every morning. His big white water dish flushes upstairs, and then the water shower runs for a while, and then we hear this buzzing noise that I don't understand, and then Robert comes down smelling like flowers.

So we're waitin' at the stairs and I turn to my buddy and ask. "Ok, Meat whose turn is it?"

Meatloaf looked away. "It's your turn."

"I don't think so, I did it last time."

"You sure?"

"Yeah," I said. "It's your turn."

"I'm tired of it."

I bumped him with my butt. "Come on. You know how Robert loves it."

"It's embarrassing."

"We gotta."

He sighed. "Ok."

When Robert came down, he looked at us both and said:

Who wants to eat?

Meatloaf bounced up and down and did a complete spin, then stood and wagged his tail all crazy-like.

Alright, let's get your food!

Meatloaf looked at me and we followed Robert as he got two cups of dog food and put it in our bowls. We crunched away, but near the bottom of my bowl, I stopped eating and carried the last mouthful out to Whiskey.

Then I ran back inside to watch so I wouldn't miss anything.

Robert burned his bread a little, and then he burnt his water a lot. He cooked it in a pot until it turned black. Weird. I've tasted some when he spilled it on the floor, and I don't get why he likes it, but it seems real important to him.

Most mornings he makes chicken eggs, and sometimes bacon. Sometimes the bacon gets dropped on the floor. Sometimes I beat Meat to it, mostly not. That dog is focused.

Robert watched his computer television until it was time to leave for work. I'm sure exactly what he does at work, but I think it's something involving money. Meatloaf says he works at a bank. I'm not sure what a bank is, but Winston said it's the place where they keep all the money.

Sometimes they try to give you money, but only if you don't need any. But if you ever go there because you really need some money, they won't give you any. It doesn't make sense to me, but I'm only a Labrador.

I find the regular morning routine around here comforting, except for that leavin' me alone part. But I know Robert will come home at nighttime.

Robert said he'd be back and walked out to his garage. We watched with our heads hangin' like we would never see him again. Robert looked sad to leave us, but I suppose he had to get to work and not give money away.

When his Jeep drove off, my buddy asked about our guest.

"Ok," Meatloaf said. "What's up? I saw you out there talking to Whiskey. How's he doing?"

"He's getting' better. When Gizmo gets here, we're gonna follow the path Whiskey took to get to our house. I'm hoping I can pick up the scent of the bag."

That reminded me of something.

"Hey Meat. I need to smell somethin' made out of leather so I can pick up the right scent on the trail."

Meatloaf sniffed in disdain. "Good luck finding anything made of natural materials in this house. It's all plastic and nylon and polyester. In fact, the only thing natural is the granite kitchen counter tops. I'm surprised Robert doesn't have plastic counter tops."

I never heard of those, but apparently my buddy didn't like them. "Meatloaf. Plastic is natural. It's made from oil, and oil comes from the earth."

Meatloaf scratched his ribs. "My human in Fresno had Mexican tile counter tops. Can't get more natural than that."

I wanted to tell Meatloaf I didn't understand this natural materials thing at all, but I didn't have time to argue. I needed to smell some leather before Gizmo and Roxie got there.

"Go up and look in Robert's closet," Meatloaf suggested. "Maybe there's some natural leather in there. Check the shoes."

I ran up real quick and went in Robert's bedroom closet. He had plenty of shoes, but I didn't know which ones were real leather. I stopped lookin' and went to the top of the stairs and barked at my friend.

"Hey Meat! What's leather smell like?"

He thought a minute. "Like a dead cow."

I was about to ask him what cow was, but then I had a better idea. I had heard of leather shoes before. I grabbed Robert's black shiny shoe in my mouth and took it downstairs. I dropped it in front of Meatloaf.

"Is that leather?" I asked him.

He sniffed it carefully. "Yeah. There's some leather there. But there's also his rayon sock and cotton shoe laces and chemical shoe polish and some dead human skin. Those extra scents might throw you off. Maybe you ought to smell one of his leather belts. Look around for a pants belt."

I took the shoe back upstairs and went lookin' for a belt. By now I had an idea of leather smell, and I found a black belt hangin' up with just that scent. I stood there and smelled it until I had a good memory. Then I went downstairs, careful not to leave any Labrador evidence behind.

Hey, I'm not a sneaky egg-sucking dog, I'm just resourceful.

I told Meatloaf. "I found a leather belt, thanks for the idea."

Yip Yip, Yip Yip

I turned my head at the sound of a small dog barking outside. "They're here," I told Meatloaf. I ran out the dog door to the side gate, just in time to see Gizmo jump over and land soft as a bird.

"Hey Dog," he said. "You ready?"

"Yeah. Roxie coming?"

"I'm out here, let me in," her voice called from the front yard.

Gizmo bounced up and flipped the latch to let Roxie in. She walked inside with a bag of something that looked like food in her mouth. She dropped it at my feet.

"Trailmix for your friend."

I nodded, then pointed toward the rear yard with my nose. "Come meet Whiskey."

We trotted back and I made the pooch introductions. Roxie brought her food with her. "It's not much," she said to Whiskey. "But it will fill you up. Sorry about my drool all over it."

Whiskey seemed to appreciate it. "That's great. Are you guys gonna look for my collar bag?"

"We are," said Gizmo. "What can you tell us about it?"

"Not much, I'm afraid. It was dark when my master tied it on. He didn't show it to me anyway. He just said he'd come back for me."

We looked at each other but didn't say anything. It sounded like Whiskey's master was a real loser. None of our humans would abandon us.

"That's all right," I said. "We know it's leather, that helps a lot."

Meatloaf came out and stood with us and said hello. He had a sleepy look on his face, but that was his normal look in the mornin'.

Roxie nudged him. "You coming with us?"

"Nah. I'm staying here. It's almost time for Paula's Home Cooking."

Gizmo cocked his head.

Meatloaf explained. "The Food Network. Paula Deen. You never seen her show? Today she's making fried mac and cheese."

"Sounds great buddy, we'll go ahead," I said. "Later Whiskey."

We walked single file out of our yard, right past old man Crenshaw's place. I looked but I didn't see him, and I hoped he didn't see us. We ran once we got to the park, we ran all the way over to the drainage pipe that would lead us out to the desert. There were a couple of city workers taking a nap next to their grass-shortening machine, but they didn't bother us.

Once we got to the other side of the drainpipe, we stopped and looked around. I didn't see anything threatening, but I didn't expect to during the day. I put my nose down and sniffed deep. I picked up a recent Quail family—a mother and a father and four or five babies—and some lizard scents, but also Whiskey's scent from days ago.

"The trail starts here," I told my two friends. "Follow me. And watch out for those jumping cactus, don't even get near one."

I took off at a fast clip, Gizmo right behind and then Roxie, their short legs movin' in a blur to keep up with me. The trail led around the million brittlebrush and scattered cholla right back to the rear of Robert's house, just like I knew it would. I looked in and saw Whiskey in the dog house watchin' us.

We went right by my house, but paused at Harley's yard next door. We barked at his sleepin' black lump on the back patio until he woke up and barked back at us.

BOW WOW

YIP YIP

WOOF WOOF

BOW WOW

YIP YIP

WOOF WOOF

BOW WOW

YIP YIP

WOOF WOOF

You know, like that.

After barking we felt energized, so we kept going, following Whiskey's scent as it swung farther out in the desert, away from the line of homes bordering the open land. Finally Gizmo called out and stopped me.

"Taser!" he said. "Are you picking up any leather bag smell?"

I sniffed deep and thought about it, eliminating the Creosote bush smell and the winter grasses sprouting up all around us. "Nope. Nothin' but Whiskey. If he had a bag on his collar, he lost it before this section of trail."

Roxie panted as we stood next to a Palo Verde tree and caught our breath. "Taser, you said something about Whiskey staying under a tree." She looked around. "But there are so many of them."

Roxie was right, but I knew a little more than she did. "He said it was a big Mesquite close to the road." We looked in the direction of the highway with all the cars and trucks that went to the Phoenix town.

"If you're worried I'm gonna miss the leather smell, don't be. Leather is too unusual out here. Let's just follow Whiskey's scent."

We were just about leave when Roxie stepped closer to the green tree trunk and stared at some scratches. She put her nose close, then stepped away.

I didn't see anything unusual, so I asked her. "What is it, Roxie?"

She motioned with her nose. "Those scratches on the tree trunk, right here. You see?"

There were long raking claw marks cutting through the thin green bark. "I see 'em."

"That's how they mark their territory."

"Who?"

"Wildcats. It's an old mark. I don't smell him, but it's definitely a bobcat. We need to be careful. He could be close by."

EIGHT

Close by…

The bobcat had ranged two miles around his new territory before the previous sunset, but now he slept fitfully under the overgrown Mesquite. The tree branches surrounding him were thick from rain running off the nearby roadway. The secluded open space under the large tree provided a safe haven for the predator to rest. It was not to be his permanent home, but it would function well as a den while he sought food.

The night's hunt had not been successful, but that was not unusual. A bobcat could go days on end without eating. When prey was finally found, he would gorge himself by simply eating more than normal. During the lean times, the hunter preferred to kill larger prey, where he would eat his fill and return later to eat more.

Now the predator hunkered down in his shelter den, one of several he needed along the perimeter of his large territory. These were necessary because his home den was miles away under a granite outcropping at the base of the mountain. He would make the trip home only after taking nourishment. The bobcat planned to find a meal close by, close to the human houses where the smell of available prey was strong.

He flexed and exposed his sharp claws as he rested, thinking of his last kill. Hunger pains gnawed at him as he tried to sleep. Soon enough, he knew, a careless animal would stumble into his path and succumb to the rage of his deadly claws and vicious teeth.

They always did.

***

I stopped in my tracks along the trail and bent down to get a better whiff of some fresh poop. I was more cautious since we found bobcat markings. "Roxie! Check this out." I already thought I knew, but I wanted her to tell me.

She bent over to smell it herself. "It's bobcat."

"The same scent we picked up at our park?"

"Yep."

"Let me smell it." Gizmo pushed by us and put his nose down next to the animal feces dropped right in the middle of the trail. He looked at me real serious. "Maybe we ought to go back home."

Gizmo was no wimpy puppy, he was one of the toughest mutts in our pack—but he wasn't stupid, either. "Maybe just a little further," I said. "We're all the way out here. It's gonna be tough to get back."

"But is it worth the risk?" Roxie asked. "What are we looking for? Human money. Useless jewelry. They're not important to dogs."

That seemed true at the moment, but Winston had said it was a matter of life and death for some human. I just didn't know who.

Gizmo didn't want to abandon me, I could tell.

He flexed the bulging muscles in his chest. "If you're going, I'm going. Two dogs are safer than one."

That was true, but I couldn't ask Gizmo to risk his life for my quest.

"No. You guys stay here. I'm only gonna go a little farther ahead. I won't do anything stupid."

Roxie and Gizmo looked at each other but didn't say anything.

"I promise."

My definition of stupid was different than their definition, but I could sense danger even before I could smell it. I took off down the trail, dodging a cholla jumping cactus that had grown close to the trail.

As I moved closer to the highway, both of my sense and smell triggers went off. The hairs on my back bristled and I stopped movin' for a moment, then continued on cautiously. The bobcat had walked the trail I was on not very long ago, sometime earlier that same day.

His musky scent clung to the bushes and grass that lined the trail. My caution turned to fear and slowed my step even more, but I had to go on, I had to see. I moved as slow as a cunning cat stalking a bird.

Something was wrong, I could feel myself trembling.

Finally, I saw the tree. It had to be the one Whiskey told me about, a big, overgrown Mesquite close to the highway. I walked closer, concentrating on the smells all around me. I tried to concentrate on what was ahead of me.

Whiskey's scent was there, yes, but an even stronger smell almost covered it up. This scent stopped me from going any closer, for I knew an enemy had taken over Whiskey's old spot.

The bobcat was nesting under the big Mesquite tree.

I stood frozen, waiting to see if the predator had seen me. No. I was safe for the moment. I should have turned and run away, but I had to be sure my nose wasn't fooling me. There was another scent under the tree. I had to be sure the other scent I caught was not my imagination. I sifted through the desert greenery smell and the rank odor of bobcat, runnin' them through my memory brain until I was sure.

Catcrap.

The other smell was leather. This was the worst possible thing. The leather bag was under Whiskey's tree with the bobcat.

Sad, but satisfied I'd learned enough, I turned to leave. I put one paw in front of the other—slowly, stealthily—so I wouldn't disturb the threat under the tree. When there was more distance between us, I broke into a trot, and then I ran.

I ran all the way back to Gizmo and Roxie. When I reached the spot where they were waiting I still didn't feel safe. I glanced back to make sure the bobcat wasn't following me.

"Let's get out of here," I said, and quickly led the way through the desert.

We didn't slow down until we were in sight of the park. Finally Gizmo stopped me in the middle of the trail.

"Taser! What happened, dog? Did you spot him?" Gizmo asked.

I stood there panting. "Yeah. I found Whiskey's tree. I think I found the leather pouch. But I found the bobcat, too. He's under the tree with the pouch."

"Yow! That's terrible. What can we do about that?"

I waited, thinking, calming down and trying to come up with a solution. "I don't think there's anything we can do. We better tell Whiskey."

We trotted into the park. Once there, Roxie and Gizmo decided they should go home, which left me to bring the bad news. I walked by Crenshaw's house lost in thought. I didn't notice whether his stupid cat was out, or if Crenshaw saw me—but I didn't care. I slipped through my gate and went right back to the doghouse. Meatloaf was layin' in the sun on the grass. He got up and came over when he saw me.

"Any luck?" Meatloaf asked.

"Yeah, bad luck." I turned to Whiskey. "I got a smell of the leather jewelry bag. I guess it fell off your neck when you were under the tree resting."

"That's great!" Whiskey said. He looked at me and on the ground at my feet. "Where is it?"

I hated to disappoint our new friend. "I'm sorry, it's still under the tree. I can't get to it. A bobcat is guarding it."

"A bobcat?"

"He's moved in under your tree. He won't stay there forever, but he'll be close by—hunting food, probably. If we try to get to it, we may run into a hungry predator. I think you better forget it, Whiskey."

He hung his head and looked at his front paws. "I thought if I found the bag, my master might find me and take me home. Now, I'll probably never see him again."

I didn't mention he might be better off without a robber criminal for a human, but I didn't think it was a good time to bring it up.

"Give it a few days, Whiskey. You never know what might happen."

As soon as that came out of my trap, I regretted it.

NINE
Inside the House, Puppy Training

When Robert came home from work and started cleaning, I knew we weren't going to the park that evening.

He opened the double front-door and the big glass back-door, and then got the leaf blower from the garage. Meatloaf ran outside right away, but I stayed to watch the fun. As soon as he turned on the blower, papers and dust flew all over the room like a hot-time Arizona dust storm inside the house.

He started at the far end and moved all the bad stuff toward the doors. A lot of the stuff flyin' around was Black Labrador hair, there musta been a million of those. It got so crazy in there I ran outside myself. Meatloaf was all the way out by the fence, but he came over when he saw me.

Whiskey poked his nose out of his house. "What's going on?"

Meat and I looked at each other. "Robert's cleanin' the house. Must be someone comin' over for dinner tonight."

"A visitor?" Whiskey asked. "Will I have to leave?"

"No, no. It's probably just Shannon, the female who lives across the street. Sometimes she comes over for dinner and to watch the television." But then I realized that could be a problem. "Catcrap. She's gonna bring Rascal over."

"Who's that?"

"It's her puppy, a crazy Yellow Lab. He's a good dog, but he gets into everything. I'll try to keep him away from you, but don't worry. He's harmless."

Meatloaf didn't agree. "I don't know, dog. What if Rascal comes out and barks at Whiskey?"

64

"We'll have to go out with him and let him know it's ok. Better yet, I'll tell him we have a friend stayin' in our backyard."

I looked up as Robert emerged from the back door with the leaf blower sprayin' air.

"Quick! Back up!" I told Whiskey, and got in front of him in the doorway of the dog house to hide him. I closed my eyes when the blower dust came by.

Robert was so busy cleanin' he didn't even look at me. He just blew the dust and dog hairs from the house right off the patio. When he was done, he wound the blower wire up and went back in the house.

"Stay in there," Meatloaf said. "He's not done cleaning."

Meat was right. Robert came out again with a little shovel and a bag to pick up our dog poop. It took him a while because of the extra stuff from Whiskey. For a minute I thought he would notice Whiskey's strange-looking poop, but he didn't seem to care. I'm sure he's seen weird poop in the back yard before. You never know what's gonna come out of Meatloaf's butt.

"All clear," I told Whiskey, and stepped out.

"He looks like a nice master, " Whiskey said sadly. "You're lucky. My human drinks alcohol and then yells at me."

I thought it was a good time to bring something up. "Whiskey, maybe we could help you find a new human."

He seemed to consider that. "But who would want an old dog with a bad leg?"

Whiskey had a point. When I was in the dog pound, I always saw the young healthy dogs find a home first. "Maybe our pack could help you find a home. All together, we know a lot of people in the neighborhood."

Whiskey sat up at the news. "That would be great! I'd love to live in this neighborhood."

"Let me work on it," I said. "We can talk later, but we gotta go inside and get ready for our dinner guests, Shannon and Rascal."

***

When the doorbell rang later, we knew who it was, there wasn't any reason to bark…except it's fun.

WOOF WOOF BOW WOW

BOW WOW WOOF WOOF

I heard a puppy bark outside in response.

Yip Yip Yip

Robert opened the door and a yellow blur ran in, all flailing legs and floppy tongue. Shannon's crazy pup ran up to us at full speed, then slid on past on the smooth tile floor. Meatloaf sidestepped the hyper Yellow Lab as it went by.

"Hi kid," I said.

He spun around to face us, excited in a way that reminded me of how wonderful it was to be young and innocent. "Hi Mister Taser! Hi Mister Meat!"

Shannon came in next carrying a dish of something that smelled like tomatoes and cheese and pasta, which was a bunch of stuff that Meat and I weren't very interested in. They probably planned it that way so we wouldn't beg…much.

Meatloaf says that smelly pasta stuff is Italy food from the country of Italy, which is not far from the country of New York, I think, because Robert's first mate Judy was from Italy and from New York. She wasn't much of a cook, but at least she could cook water without burning it black.

Rascal didn't seem interested in the food Shannon brought either. He ran over and looked up at me like I was his hero.

"Can you tell me some more human stuff, Mister Taser? Huh? Can you?"

"Sure thing, kid."

I'd been trying to bring Shannon's puppy up to speed on what you have to do to survive in the human world. The important things came naturally to dogs, but the best stuff had to be taught. Most dogs don't have any idea of what they can learn if they just listen to humans, except when they talk about politics.

I had him sit down. "Let's go over food and mealtime. We already told you about putting on a big show to reinforce human feeding behavior."

Rascal panted. "Yeah, I get all crazy excited when they feed me. One time I even peed on the floor."

"Hmmm. That may be overdoing it. It might be better to save peeing on the floor for when people come over. Now, this is a little different. It's about the quality of food they give you. See, not all food is the same. Meat, you better tell him." I turned back to the puppy. "Mister Meat is the pack food expert."

Meatloaf spoke up. "Right now your humans are giving you puppy chow, Right? Eukanuba puppy formula?"

"Right. How do you know that?"

"I can smell it on your breath. Natural Lamb and Rice."

"Wow."

Meatloaf got this real serious look on his face. Which isn't easy for a Labrador, unless you're thinking about eating.

"Pretty soon they're gonna switch your puppy food to adult food," Meatloaf said. "Don't let them go cheap on you. If they try and give you some cheap brand with a lot of cereal filler in, just turn up your nose and walk away."

"You want me to walk away from my food?"

"That's right. You'll only have to do it once or twice, and they'll get all upset that you're not eating. They'll feel terrible and they'll run out and buy you the good stuff."

"Thanks, Mister Meat."

"How are you doing on your human words?" I asked him.

"I been watching their television picture," Rascal said. "But I get tired of it. It's so boring. Why do they watch it?"

"They got nothin' else to do at night," I explained. "Besides, they don't know how to think, unless some talking head on the television news tells 'em what's goin' on."

Rascal looked serious. "Those male news-humans scare me. I like the females, though. They're cute, like me."

I wasn't gonna tell him that all dogs were cute when they're puppies, but when they grow up they're just another mutt.

"Alright, kid. The important thing is not to make it obvious you're watching their television. You don't want to let them know how smart you are. So here's what you do. Let's say you're watching television, and a show comes on with a dog in it."

The puppy jumped up. "Yeah, I've seen those! Little dog shows where they feed the dog in the kitchen!" He wagged his tail.

"Right," I said. I didn't have the heart to tell Rascal those were television commercials. I try to spare him the ugly parts of life. "When that happens your human will point at the television and say, 'Look Rascal, a dog!' But don't look at the television picture, look at their hand. And they'll keep pointing and saying, 'Look at the dog, look at the dog', but don't do it. Just look at their hand, or at their face, like you don't understand. They'll give up and think you're just a dumb mutt."

"That sounds like fun."

"Then, when they go back to watching their television, you keep listening to human talk."

"I got it."

"Now. Are you having any trouble with their words?"

He scratched behind his ear, then said, "A couple. What's politics?"

I knew it would be hard to explain to a puppy, so I thought a minute. "It's like wrestling for people who went to college."

"What's wrestling?"

"You see it on television. That channel with humans rolling around on the floor with hardly any clothes on, grunting and groaning."

"You mean HBO?"

I didn't think that was it. "Maybe Shannon doesn't watch it. What other words give you trouble?"

"Clock. She has this clock by her bed."

"That's how humans know when to wake up and go to work. What else?"

"Naps. I don't understand that word."

"Naps? That's what humans call sleeping on the couch."

"I keep hearing all this talk about naps."

"Your human has to tell you to take naps?" Meatloaf looked puzzled. "Nobody ever had to tell me to take naps."

"She's not talking about sleeping, it's something else," Rascal said. "Shannon says she has to 'download a nap'. It's always, downloadanap, downloadanap. It makes me crazy."

I scratched my ribs and thought. "I can't help you there, but I think it has to do with those little boxes they love so much. Anything else?"

"Yeah. I have a question. What is this sack for?" Rascal rolled over on his back and spread his legs. "When I sniff female dogs, I see they don't have a sack with two round things in it. Does that mean we're special?"

This much I knew all about. "All males have those, not just Labrador males" I explained. "Robert's last mate, Judy, talked about this. As I understand it, those round nuts are male brains. I think males have to keep their brains out in the open air so they stay cool."

Rascal seemed confused with this new information. "Does that mean females don't have brains?"

"Not at all. They keep their brains hidden inside their body to fool the males into thinking females are dumber. It's something that happened when we evolved many years ago."

"Females are smarter than us?"

"The sooner you accept that, kid, the easier your life will be. Just don't tell the pack I told you so."

Rascal looked down between his legs again. "But I see two nuts. Do males have two brains?"

"No, we've got two halves. When you get older, you'll hear humans talk about right-brain stuff and left-brain stuff. The right brain is your creative side, while the left side does the serious thinking. Or maybe it's the other way around."

The pup looked worried. "My lumps seem awful small for brains."

"Sure, males have small brains, but they're powerful. We can do a lot of damage with those little nuts."

Meatloaf brought up an important tip. "Remember to keep them clean. When I lick my brains, they work better." He thought a minute. "It feels like they work better, anyway."

"Gosh. You guys know everything."

"Stick with us, kid. Mister Meat and I have been all the way around the block. Now, I have something important to discuss with you, dog to dog."

Rascal's tale wagged furiously. "You mean about mounting females?"

I was amazed at what came out of the pup's mouth. "How do you know about that?"

"Mister Meat told me."

I looked down my nose at Meatloaf. "Meat. What've you been tellin' the kid, here?"

Meatloaf shrugged. "Nothing much. Winston and I just gave him a few female tips."

I looked back at Rascal. "No, pup. You're still too young to worry about that stuff, don't pay any attention to Mister Meat's stories. And don't talk to Mister Winston about mounting anymore, he's not normal. He's from England."

Rascal looked disappointed. "So what did you want to talk about?"

I looked to one side, then the other, making a big deal out of it. "It's a secret."

"Yea!"

"Let's go outside."

70

I led Rascal to the laundry room and the dog door. I went out first and headed to the back, but when I turned around, Rascal wasn't there. I started to go back inside to find him, but just then Rascal stepped out the dog door with a cotton sock in his mouth.

"Look what I found!"

I shook my head. "That's Robert's sock. We don't chew his stuff or we get, *No, No Bad Dog.*"

"I hate when they say that." Rascal dropped it and followed me. He stopped to lift his leg on a bush, and then once again on the wall, and then he ran up to meet me by the dog house. He took a step back when Whiskey poked his head out the door.

"Woof!" Rascal blurted out. "Who are you?"

"I'm Whiskey."

Rascal stepped forward and sniffed cautiously.

I motioned with my snout. "Whiskey is our secret. He's staying with us for a while, but Robert doesn't know. Whiskey hurt his leg and needs food."

Rascal hung his head. "But I don't have any food."

"It's alright pup, just keep it a secret. Don't bark when you're out here, we don't want to attract Robert or Shannon and have them find our friend."

"Ok." Rascal cocked his head and spoke to Whiskey. "Where's your master? Why doesn't he feed you?"

"I lost him."

"Why doesn't he look and find you? When I'm lost, Shannon comes to look for me. And I get lost a lot."

This was not helping our pathetic friend, so I wanted to get the puppy back in the house. "Whiskey's master is away on a trip. We're helping while he's gone. But I think we ought to go inside now."

"Ok. Bye, Mister Whiskey." Rascal turned to me as we were trottin' back to the dog door. "You sure I can't have that sock?"

"Sorry."

I took the sock back inside, wondering why I ever thought Rascal's concern would be a strange dog in out backyard.

We looked for Meatloaf in the living room, but found him in the kitchen staring at Robert and Shannon. The sharp smell of parmesan cheese and garlic filled the air. Our humans were leaning against the counter drinking beer from bottles.

You can't miss the beer smell, because there isn't anything that smells like it. One time Robert spilled some and I started to lick it, but then decided it was too strange. Meatloaf took care of it for me.

So we were all in the kitchen, but my buddy was right at the feet of our masters. They were busy munching on bread and butter. Meatloaf says the Food Channel is always talkin' about France bread—from the country of France. Apparently there's the country of Italy and there's the country of France, and they have their own different food. So it didn't make sense to me that they had France bread with Italy food, but maybe Robert and Shannon got confused thinking 'cause they were drinking beer. I'd seen that before.

Anyway Meat looked like he wanted some of that bread, no matter where it came from.

I bumped Rascal. "Now watch how Mister Meat does this."

Meatloaf locked eyes with Robert as he talked with Shannon. Robert moved a couple steps closer to the oven to check the dinner. Meatloaf moved his position too, so Robert couldn't avoid his piercing stare. Finally Robert looked down, then handed Meatloaf a slice of France bread, which disappeared immediately.

"Cool," Rascal said.

"Yeah. They can't stand it when you stare at them."

Rascal watched the scene closely. "Why not?"

"They're guilty. They know they get to eat whenever they want, but they only feed us twice a day. So they use some excuse about not wanting us to get fat, or how they don't want to spoil us, or some other lie."

"Lie? What's a lie?"

"It's something humans do," I said. "It's what they call it when they don't tell you what's really happening."

"Do dogs lie?"

"No."

Rascal cocked his head. "Why not?"

"We can't."

Rascal cocked his head in the other direction. "Why not?"

That was a good question, but I didn't have an answer. I thought about how Whiskey had tried to lie about what happened to him, but then admitted the truth. And I thought of all the times I wanted to lie but couldn't.

"I don't know why dogs can't lie. It's something inside us, we just can't."

***

It was totally dark when the bobcat left his safe shelter under the Mesquite tree to hunt, determined now to kill and satisfy his hunger. He prowled under the cover of night, confidant his stealthy form would not be seen by his prey until it was too late. He was a cunning hunter, a creature who was seldom seen before he struck. He killed so swiftly that his victims only had a fleeting glimpse before they died.

The bobcat threaded his way between cactus and bush toward the nearby human houses. The houses were brightly lit and loud, but the wildcat was not afraid, only wary. This night, hunger drove him toward his best chance of success.

He sifted scents as he walked. He picked up the stale odor of rabbit, a rabbit now gone and safely burrowed in. A field rodent had nibbled the grass along the trail, and then disappeared. But tonight the bobcat was not interested in small prey, he would search out larger victims, and he knew where he would find one.

He stepped down into the desert sand wash that followed the line of human houses until he saw the two-story home he had visited before.

The normal nightly noise drifted out to greet him. Repeated exposure had taught the wildcat that humans were not to be feared, only respected. It was only an ancient warning in his brain that urged caution, nothing in this animal's experience gave him pause. He had found prey among the humans before, and humans had never offered resistance. He expected none now.

He jumped out of the wash and walked closer—slowly, cautiously, sifting new scents at the two-story house. The wounded dog was there, yes, but there were other dogs about and two humans present. The bobcat could see their forms through rear windows.

Maybe this was not the moment to strike after all. He paused, ears twitching from the noise and laughter coming from inside, then he hissed in anger. No. This was not his night to get the wounded dog.

He turned and continued walking along the back of the houses. This was the second time he'd lost the opportunity and his frustration grew. He needed to eat.

Not all the houses were lit, not all held the promise of food, but a faint scent from the rear yard of the second house caught his attention.

The bobcat jumped gracefully to the top of the block fence post and peered though the darkness. Yes. He saw prey here. It was not as big as the wounded dog, but it was fat and it was available. His potential victim lay casually on its side on the concrete patio, totally unaware of an imminent threat.

The bobcat assessed the risk.

Something flickered and murmured quietly behind drawn curtains. The weak light filtered out to the back yard and illuminated his careless prey. This was the opportunity he wanted. This was what the human houses offered—lazy pets oblivious to the dangers of the wild.

The bobcat coiled his leg muscles and prepared to launch, his black nose forward, his four paws close together on the block post. Fifteen feet away, the chubby Burmese cat licked his fur, intent only on his daily cleaning ritual.

The bobcat launched silently into the air.

When the killer landed on him, the Burmese never knew what struck him. Razor sharp claws dug into his spine as sharp teeth penetrated his skull. The bobcat bit down hard until his victim did not twitch or moan.

Enraged by his kill, the bobcat clawed and ripped into the furry pet right there on the patio. Scraps of the feline were either eaten or discarded as warm blood flowed in the cold December night.

TEN
Taser in Trouble

I woke up early, but I didn't move anything except my eyes. Sometimes I do that, just lie there on the floor and stare straight ahead, thinkin' about stuff that happened. The Animal Channel says dogs live in the present moment, but I spend a lot of time worrying about next moments, or worrying about other dogs. It could be I'm special.

It could be I'm strange.

I hated to give up the search for Whiskey's lost jewelry bag, but it didn't seem worth the risk anymore. Besides, I thought a better plan was to try and find Whiskey a new master. There had to be some human besides a robber criminal for him. I made a memory to talk to the pack about it that night.

The truth was, I was a little tired from entertainin' Rascal all night. When Shannon and her puppy finally left, I was glad to see them go. Meatloaf went to bed early. He probably wanted to get away from all the puppy questions.

We finally got some leftovers when they cleaned the kitchen after dinner. I even took some to Whiskey. We had some of that bread, which is one of my favorite foods, along with all my other favorite foods, which is anything they'll give me. I was thinkin' of food and my first meal when I heard a knock.

BANG BANG BANG.

Actually, it was louder than a knock, which meant it was probably Mister Crenshaw again.

BANG BANG BANG.

I think Robert thought it was Mister Crenshaw too, because he stopped and gave me that *'what have you been up to now?'* look before he opened the door. I didn't go near the front this time, me and Meatloaf stood way back so Crenshaw wouldn't see us.

They stood there talkin' a while.

Your dog…

Right away I knew that didn't sound good.

My cat…last time…animal control…intolerable…neighbors…dog pound…

Ok, I knew what dog pound meant, so it was sounding even worse

Roaming neighborhood…police…rules…last night…blood…

All of a sudden I understood what happened. He went on and on, but I quit listening. Then Robert started arguing with him. I think he was sticking up for me.

Even Meatloaf got interested. "What's he saying, Taser?"

"Something ate Crenshaw's stupid cat last night."

"That's good."

"Crenshaw thinks it was me."

"That's bad."

"It's dumb. Dogs don't eat cats." I thought a minute. "Do they?"

"Nah. They might chew on 'em a while, but they don't swallow them. It had to be a coyote. They love swallowing cats."

"He's talkin' about callin' the animal control people on us."

Meatloaf backed up a little. "Us? What'd ya mean, us?"

"Don't get excited. Robert doesn't believe we ate anybody's cat."

Meatloaf pointed at the door with his snout. "That's not just anybody, that's the head of the homeowners association. Those guys can send you to prison."

"Well, he's not sendin' me to any prison, or the dog pound either."

"He doesn't like you, Taser. It's personal with him. Remember when he caught you in the garage chasing his cat?"

I remembered.

Meatloaf told me anyway. "You attacked his precious cat. That's the problem."

"Oh? What about you and that steak?"

"You were the one he saw with it in your mouth."

"What is it with that guy?"

"Crenshaw? He lost his pet. That would upset anyone."

"Yeah. I guess that would make you mad." I almost felt sorry for the guy. "But he doesn't have to take it out on me."

I spent the rest of the morning talking to Whiskey, and I decided he was a great dog who'd had a rough life, just like me. He'd had different masters and none of them seemed to pay much attention to him. He certainly wasn't a bad dog.

I snuck him a whole package of muffins from the pantry. He really liked those, but who wouldn't? I think the food helped him get stronger.

After that we spent some time sleepin' in the sun, which musta felt good to him after a cold night in the dog house.

As the day passed, I got anxious about tellin' Winston I was through with the lost bag search. I probably shoulda kept my big mouth shut. So I was less than thrilled about goin' to the park, but glad to get it over. I wanted to get back to normal dog stuff for a while.

Either way, Robert came home as usual and the decision was out of my paws.

After dinner, he went to the drawer and pulled out two leashes. Personally, I don't mind being on a leash for a while, it makes me feel special. As long as I get loose at the park it's no big deal. I like to be free to sniff poop, 'cause I know that activity makes humans nervous. They don't know what they're missin'.

He clipped the blue leash on Meatloaf and the red leash on me. At least Robert calls it red, I wouldn't know. The Animal Channel says human red looks like yellow to a dog, but I'd like to know how they figured that out. Personally I don't believe it matters. I like to think it's humans who can't see our colors, instead of the other way around.

So we walked to the park on our leash right by Mister Crenshaw's place all nice and legal and obedient, but when we reached the park Robert let us free. The first thing I did was lift my leg on a couple of my favorite bushes. It's not that I had to go that bad, but whenever I smell some other dog's pee it makes me want to go there too. Some stuff I do because my right brain tells me. Or is that my left brain?

I looked around for Simba, but I couldn't see or smell her. Gizmo was out chasin' his tennis ball for his master, so I joined in. I only got the ball once, because Gizmo's Jack Russell legs can run circles around me. The muscular little guy is fast. After a while we tired out his master and trotted over to join the pack.

I saw Remi and Winston and Roxie. I trotted up to Winston and sniffed hello.

The English Bulldog spoke first. "How's Whiskey?"

"He's gettin' better," I said. "He can walk with a limp, but it's not as bad as when he first came to stay."

"Excellent. Now, what manner of luck have you had in the search? I must tell you Taser, my friend is counting on you."

I musta looked guilty, because I sure felt it. "Look Winston, I got bad news. I'm givin' up the search for the jewelry bag."

His jaw dropped. "But why?"

"It's too dangerous. I smelled the bag along Whiskey's path at a bobcat's den. He's livin' under the same tree where Whiskey hid after the robbery. It must have fallen off his collar there."

Winston's stepped closer to me, his eyes wide. "Taser, please! That bag must be returned forthwith!"

This wasn't making any sense, I couldn't figure out what the big deal was. "Why? What's so important about that stupid jewelry?"

"Uhh. Uhh. I can't tell you, Taser. You must take my word for it."

"Sorry, Winston, I can't take the risk. I don't want to tangle with any crazy bobcat. Besides, Robert is watchin' me real close now, and I'm getting' all this heat from the homeowner guy. He's after my skin."

"Yes, yes, but…"

I asked him the big question straight out. "Who owns the jewelry?"

Winston blinked. "I'm sorry. I'm sworn to secrecy."

"I understand you want me to do this, but I can't see the point anymore. We're only talkin' about human money, Winston."

"No. That's the thing you have to understand, it's not about human money. It's about a human life. And it's also about a dog's life."

This was gettin' too heavy for me. It was bad enough takin' care of Whiskey, now they expected me to carry the neighborhood.

"Sorry. Unless I know more, I can't take any chances. I'm just a dog, Winston."

Remi sniggered. "Finally, Taser admits he's not superpooch."

"Shutup, Remi," Meatloaf growled.

"Don't listen to Remi," Gizmo said, "that's just the Tasty Treats talking."

Winston objected to my decision. "Please, you must reconsider your…"

I held up my paw. I didn't want to argue with the Bulldog about it. Winston sat down on his beefy haunches with a face that drooped more than normal.

Then Remi started to needle me about my predicament. "What's the matter, Taser? You scared of a big pussy cat? I thought you'd jump at the chance to meddle in animal affairs."

Remi was one mutt in the pack who didn't appreciate my efforts. But I knew Gizmo and Meatloaf understood.

So did Roxie. "Leave Taser alone, Remi."

Remi sniffed. "Well. Personally, I think it's about time the homeowner's association put a stop to our neighborhood pest. Taser always brings us trouble. With his record, it's amazing no one's been killed lately."

Meatloaf spoke up. "That's not true, numb-nuts. Old man Crenshaw's Burmese cat got killed last night. Killed and eaten."

"Oh my word. What manner of predator was responsible?"

"My guess is it was a coyote. I suppose it could have been the bobcat."

"A wildcat eating a house cat?" Roxie said. "That would be cannibalism, wouldn't it?"

"No, that would be catabalism," Gizmo cracked.

"Honestly." Remi turned away. "I do not find this amusing."

Meatloaf kept it up. "I suppose after he digests that Burmese food, he'll be coming to your house to try a little French cuisine. He probably won't like the taste. French food gives me gas."

"You idiots disgust me." Remi turned and walked away in a huff.

I took the opportunity to bring up my new idea. "I'm hopin' the pack can help Whiskey find a new master. He's a great pooch. I think he'd be a perfect companion for a human couple in our neighborhood."

"My neighbor doesn't have a dog, and he thinks I'm cool." Roxie said. "Except they have little kids."

"So? Kids love dogs, that might work."

"But not all humans are friendly. We have to face the facts, not everybody likes dogs."

I don't understand that kind of human thinking. What's not to like about dogs? Except maybe dog vomit in the house? Or a buncha dog poop in the yard? Or dog hair all over the floor? I suppose it could be the expensive vet bills or our constant beggin' to eat or go for a walk. Or maybe it was the furniture chewin' or the diggin' in the yard business.

Except for that stuff, dogs are great.

I thought I should ask Winston because he got out of the house a lot. "Hey Winston. You get around the neighborhood, what do you think? Any chance of finding a home for Whiskey?"

"Harrumphh. Quite possibly. I'll do what I can for the poor creature. In the meantime, Taser, please reconsider your decision."

"I'll think about it."

Yeah, I'd think about it, but I couldn't see what might possibly change my mind.

**

Whiskey raised one ear at the slam of the front door. Taser and Meatloaf were leaving the house with Robert to go to the park, just like they did most nights. There was no missing the excited panting as they ran across the yard and down the sidewalk. Soon after, he could hear dogs at the park bark and howl and yip hello. It sounded like a lot of fun.

He sighed.

Whiskey got up to stretch his legs, something he did several times a day to help himself heal. He stepped out and walked into the yard to pee, then sniffed around in hopes of finding something interesting or edible.

He could put more weight on the wounded back leg now, it hurt less. Whiskey limped to the rear fence so he could look out on the desert. He could hear the cars and trucks over at the big road. It reminded him of what happened the night of the robbery.

He knew something was wrong when his master went to the door of that house. He could smell the fear and anger. It had happened a couple times before. It happened once when his master was driving on the road. He got mad and swerved his car at another driver and yelled out the window.

Another time they were on a walk and a German Shepherd came up to Whiskey and went to bite him—but his master took something from his pocket and hit the dog. It yelped and ran away.

He had the same smell that night of the robbery, a smell of fear and anger, a smell like his master was going to fight. Whiskey was scared, but he followed his owner anyway. He knew he would protect him. He had saved him before.

But that night was different.

Now, Whiskey felt lost and abandoned.

He turned and walked toward the house, hoping to lift his spirit. Taser's house seemed warm and friendly. Whiskey had a sudden urge to go inside and see what it was like. He turned and hobbled along the side of the house.

He paused at the dog door. Taser told him not to go in there, but they were off at the park, so he didn't think it would matter. There was plenty of time.

Whiskey pushed the plastic door open with his head and looked in the house. The dog door opened into a small room with strong soap smells and dirty human clothes. He saw two big white machines but not much else in the room. It seemed safe to investigate, so he stepped inside and walked to the room door leading to the rest of the house.

He peered around the corner in amazement. He'd never seen a bigger, nicer home. All the furniture looked new and nice—except for those teeth marks on all the table legs. It looked comfortable and friendly, the kind of home he'd love to live in if he had a chance.

He sat down on the tile floor to think. It was beginning to look like he'd never see his master again. So many days had passed since he saw him he'd lost count of the time. Maybe Taser was right, maybe he should look for a new master.

Whiskey limped down the hall into the kitchen and sniffed the air. What was that smell? He moved toward the sink counter and sniffed again. Then he turned and walked in the pantry, examining the shelves. He could smell some wheat bread and hamburger buns on an upper shelf, but he couldn't reach it. So he turned away and went back in the main kitchen.

Sniff, sniff.

The best smells seemed to be coming from the cabinet under the sink. He walked over and pawed at the door—once, twice—and it cracked enough to get his nose in and the cabinet door opened all the way. Inside he saw a can with a plastic bag in it.

The stuff in the plastic bag smelled like old food, the stuff humans called garbage for some reason. As far as he could tell, today's garbage was just yesterday's food that smelled better. He nosed around until he found something in there he could eat, then he bit, chewed, and swallowed. He wasn't thinking about hiding or not getting caught, he was just acting like a hungry dog.

Click-click.

All of a sudden there was a noise at the door.

Uh oh.

Whiskey's head jerked sideways and the garbage can fell over and he ran. He hobbled as fast as he could to the dog door, then hurried outside and back to his dog house. He moved all the way to the rear and put his head down on his paws, hoping no one had seen the pathetic creature who just wanted something to eat.

***

Robert opened the front door and Meatloaf and I rushed to our water and slurped until we'd made a big mess of the floor. When I raised my head and licked my lips, I saw the front door was still open. Then I heard Robert talkin' to someone. I padded over to look and saw Robert had walked out in the front yard to say somethin' to Shannon across the street.

I was just about to go outside myself to get some attention from her when I heard Meatloaf call me.

"Taser."

I walked toward his voice.

"Taser!"

It sounded serious.

I found Meatloaf in the kitchen. When I walked in I saw the problem right away. The garbage pail was on its side and there was garbage all over the floor, which could only mean one thing.

Whiskey.

Meatloaf shook his head. "I'm not taking the rap for this."

I stood there thinkin' about what to do, but there was only one thing possible. "Go in the living room. I'll handle this."

When Meatloaf left, I walked to the can and looked for somethin' edible. I pulled a banana peal out and stood there with it hangin' outta my mouth.

When Robert came in he just looked at me. I hadn't gotten in the garbage since he left the can out after Thanksgiving dinner.

But this was more serious. Openin' the door and draggin' out the can?

Taser!

I dropped the banana peal hung my head and looked guilty.

Robert came over and picked up the can and the stuff on the floor. I slinked off to join Meat in the living room.

He looked over at me. "That was close. What's up with Whiskey?"

"I dunno."

"We gotta get that dog out of here, Taser. Robert's gonna find him and get mad."

"So what? What's he gonna do to us?"

"It's not you and me I'm worried about. What if he calls the animal control people and they take Whiskey to the pound?"

That would be a complete disaster. But there was somethin' worse.

"Robert could call Whiskey's master." I said. "They have those lost dog signs with Whiskey's picture all over the neighborhood. What if Robert calls the robber criminal to come get his dog and he shows up and hurts Robert? We hafta look out for our home."

Meatloaf crossed his paws. "Whiskey's gotta go. Robert comes first."

Meat was right, I understood that.

What I didn't understand, was why we were hiding from Whiskey's master. Why would he come back and risk getting caught by the police, just to get that bag?

What could be in that stupid pouch that was worth all this trouble?

ELEVEN
Philadelphia, Pennsylvania   April 5, 1933

When his stomach rumbled for the third time, Peter Carter turned around to read the wall clock behind the counter where he worked. Another thirty minutes and he'd be off to lunch to meet Dorothy at the hash diner next door. He was looking forward to seeing her for two reasons. The first was she was cute as a button. The second reason was he had no money for lunch, and sweet Dorothy was buying.

The lucky few like Peter who had a job in the Great Depression rarely wasted their money on lunch, even if they had the quarter needed for a cheese sandwich, apple pie and a glass of milk.

So when his boss, Maxwell Trumball, Director of the Philadelphia Mint, announced there would be an emergency employee meeting at twelve noon instead of their normal lunch hour, Peter's hopes for food and romance died.

He turned to his teller partner and complained. "Who put the bee under Trumball's bonnet?"

Jimmy thumbed his suspenders. "Just keep smiling, Peter. You've missed lunch before."

"But today I'm starving."

"Maybe if you didn't spend all your money collecting coins, you'd have a dollar left over for a proper meal."

Peter snorted. "Paper notes are useless, they always lose their value. Gold is the secret to financial success, my friend."

"You're an old fashioned guy, Peter. Why would anyone want to carry metal anymore?"

Peter fingered the paper dollars in his front pocket. "Because they can't print gold coins."

Jimmy snorted. "Gold is an ancient relic whose time has passed."

At precisely twelve o'clock, Peter and Jimmy closed their window and filed into the lunch room in at the rear of the building with all twenty-two U.S. Mint employees. Peter left the few available chairs for the ladies and stood close to the wall.

Maxwell Trumball stood silently in the front of his employees, heightening the tension rippling through the room. They wouldn't close the Mint, would they? Could it be that bad?

Trumball cleared his throat. "We have been directed by President Roosevelt to immediately cease the transfer of gold to the general public."

A murmur spread among them. They heard rumors something like this was coming, but this was drastic action from the new President. At least the Mint wasn't closing.

Trumball continued. "The President has issued Executive Order 6102, which forbids public hoarding of gold coin, gold bullion, and gold certificates within the continental United States. All US citizens are directed to turn in any gold or gold coins they currently possess. We expect a large influx of coins, and to a lesser extent, gold bullion. We will have the necessary procedures in place by tomorrow morning to handle this."

Peter looked over at Jimmy, but Jimmy averted his eyes.

Trumball went on. "We have already contacted our member banks and instructed them on gold transfer procedures. As far as you tellers here at the mint, please return to your windows to balance out and take all monies to the vault. The Philadelphia Mint will be closed to the public for the remainder of the day."

Peter fingered his new Federal Reserve Notes in the pocket of his pleated wool slacks. Pants pockets was where he kept his money since the banks started failing. He knew he had thirty-four dollars and seventy-five cents, enough to pay his upcoming rent payment, bills, and buy a few groceries for the month.

When he got back to his window, he eyed the stack of gold 1933 Saint Gaudens Double Eagles as he set about to balance his cash drawer. He had hoped to get a '33 Eagle to complement his collection ever since their release three weeks previous. He had one Saint Gaudens twenty-dollar gold piece for each year they'd been issued, from 1907 to 1932. His life savings was his gold coin collection, for good reason.

He kept the collection buried in a biscuit tin his grandparents backyard out in Chester Springs. Twenty paces north of the wood shed, ten paces west of the old oak, twelve inches down. Let them find that, Peter thought. He didn't plan on giving his gold to the President or anyone else. It could stay buried until he needed it for his old age.

He glanced over at Jimmy who was busy closing his own window. Jimmy didn't know anything about saving or investing, he lived for the moment. Jimmy spent all his money on bootleg gin and dance-club dollies.

Peter was more cautious, especially for a young man. His family was wiped out in the '29 stock market crash. After Peter's father lost all their money and their home, Peter swore he'd never own any piece of paper claiming a value over one cent.

For a second Peter thought about stealing the gold coin, and then he put it out of his mind. He wouldn't do anything to risk his job. Besides, he'd never get away with it, security at the Mint was too tight. More than that, he wasn't a thief and he wouldn't steal, no matter how desperate things might be.

The executive order by Roosevelt was unprecedented and it showed Peter how serious the financial state of the nation was. But it also meant there were only minutes left to decide what to do.

If he acted immediately, he could trade his paper dollars for one Double Eagle and it would show up in the morning's transactions. The only problem was the dollars in his pocket were already budgeted.

He picked one coin off the top of the stack and felt its weight, then decided he had to have it. He swapped the coin for twenty of his folded paper dollars along with sixty-seven cents, the official dollar exchange rate for one ounce of gold in April, 1933. His cash drawer would balance and he'd have one of the few 1933 Saint Gaudens Double Eagle that ever made it out to public hands.

He'd worry about his rent next month.

Eating was a different problem. But if he was correct in his thinking, sweet Dorothy wouldn't allow her future husband to starve to death anytime soon.

TWELVE
Taser on the Case

I spent a rough night struggling with my refusal to help Winston. He always helped me when I had trouble, so I felt guilty about refusing him. If only he would tell me more about the robbery.

As soon as I woke up, I decided it was time to get some answers. I waited until Robert drove off to work, then I went outside to talk to Whiskey. I wasn't mad at him for comin' in our house, he was just a dog in need. The fact that he screwed up didn't bother me, I've screwed up before. Plenty of times.

I found him awake and bright-eyed. "Hey Whiskey, how's the leg today?"

"It's good. Can I come out?"

"Sure. It's all clear."

Whiskey stood and limped out to the yard and peed, struggling a little as he did. "It's tough to lift a leg in my condition," he explained.

"I'll bet."

He looked guilty. "I'm sorry about coming inside last night. I don't know what happened to my thinking. Then I smelled the food in the kitchen and it was all over."

"Forget it." I didn't plan on tellin' Whiskey his time was runnin' short with us. I didn't have the stomach to tell him yet, and I wanted to make sure he was better.

I told him my other plan, the one that was rattlin' around in my left brain. Or maybe my right. "I'm gonna do some scouting around this mornin'. Is there anythin' more you can tell me about that robbery?"

"Like what?"

"Where it was. Or what'd the houses look like?"

"Just like these houses. It was in your neighborhood."

"Was it tall?"

"Tall?"

"Did it have a top part like ours or was it short like the one over there?"

Whiskey looked at our place and then Shannon's across the street. He nosed at Shannon's house. "Like that one."

Single story. This was good information, it narrowed down the possibilities. "Tell me about the front yard. Was it grass or this desert rock?"

"I'm pretty sure it's grass."

That wasn't much, but it was better than nothin'. I was just about to leave when Whiskey threw out the key to the whole thing.

"Taser. I've been thinking about that dog."

"What dog?"

"The dog at the robbery house, the dog that bit my master. I think I know what kind of pooch it was."

"Yeah?"

"A Doberman."

"You sure?"

"Almost positive. You know how they got those skinny snouts and big chests? Their bark has that funny high sound, you know. And the snarl is real mean. It was a Doberman. I'd bet a steak bone...if I had one."

"Whiskey, if you're right, I'll get you a steak bone."

"You know who it is?"

I thought I did. "The only Doberman in the neighborhood is Spike. His master is an older male, too."

"Yeah," Whiskey said. "He was old. Does he have those pictures on his arms?"

"Not sure about that."

"So what're you gonna do?"

I wasn't sure. But if it was Spike's house that got robbed and lost the jewelry bag, I felt kinda obligated to help him. He was a friend of the pack because he helped us find Harley. The least I could do was find out if he really was the victim.

I decided and told Whiskey. "I'm gonna go talk to Spike and see what I can find out."

Whiskey looked scared. "What if he wants his bag back? What if he comes over to bite me?"

"Spike ain't like that, I'll talk to him about our problem. You ain't got the bag, so there's nothin' you can do. I'm more concerned about finding you a home."

Whiskey nodded. "That would be great."

"I'll let you know if I have any luck."

I ran back in the house and looked for Meatloaf so I could tell him I was leavin'. He was watchin' the Food Channel and barely looked up at me. "Yeah," he said. "Ok dog. Whatever."

So I went back outside and blew the gate latch and started down the street toward Winston's place. Luckily, it's in the other direction from Crenshaw's house, so I wasn't worried. I was walkin' toward Winston's house but I was thinkin' about Spike.

Spike was kind of a friend. He helped us one time rescue Harley, so we think of Spike as an honorary member of our pack, even if he doesn't come to the park with us.

He doesn't like me much, but we got this mutual respect thing goin' on because of our different talents. He thinks I snoop around, but I think it only bugs him because he's got secrets.

Spike's master definitely has secrets. He doesn't socialize with the rest of the humans in out neighborhood or get out of the house much. Winston knows Spike pretty well. He walks by his house a lot, so he reports what's up to the pack.

Winston is convinced Spike's master is in some sort of witness protection program. He's got this heavy Brooklyn accent but he claims he's from Cottonwood, which is a little town in Arizona. It don't add up, even to a mutt. I think he's definitely on the shady side of the law any way you cut it.

The fact that Spike and Winston talk a lot makes me think he could be the robbery victim that needs help.

I didn't run, but I trotted to the end of our street and then went down two more streets toward Winston's home. I got some funny looks from a lady drivin' by in a car, but the two guys in an old grass-shortening truck didn't pay any attention to me.

The grass-shortening guys are cool, they like dogs and they're not afraid of us like some of the females. But most of them speak some strange language, I think it's French. They come around and trim and clean the neighbor's yards, but not ours, probably 'cause Robert can't speak French

I could smell all the bush branches they had in the back of their truck, I could even smell dog pee on some branches. I thought that was weird. Most humans spoil our fun by pickin' up the dog poop. It's like they got a weird bathroom problem or somethin'.

I picked up other smells as I walked, and I filed 'em away in my left brain. Or maybe my right brain, I'm not sure. Dogs got a million smells all arranged and separated into food parts of the brain and people parts of the brain, different parts like that.

Take peanut butter. That's a great food. I know, because one time Robert made a big mistake and gave me and Meat a cracker with some peanut butter on it. Now, every time he tries to sneak the lid off the peanut butter jar for a little for himself—WHAM—there's Meatloaf and me starin' at him with our tails waggin', even if we were off in the next room.

All he's gotta do is open the lid and we know. The Animal Channel says dogs only need one molecule in a billion molecules of air to pick up a smell. It might have been a trillion instead of a billion, but I don't know the difference. I heard Robert say the govament doesn't know the difference either, so I'm not the only one.

When I got to Winston's place, I went to the side yard gate so I could see through the slats. I couldn't see him but I could smell his master's cigar. So I gave a little bark.

Woof

I waited, then I gave another, this one a little louder. I figured he must be sleepin' inside.

WOOF

I heard the dog door bang and then Winston waddled up. I love lookin' at Winston's face and tryin' to figure out what went wrong with his nose and teeth. But I never say anything to him 'cause I don't want to let on that he looks weird. On the other hand, he is from England.

"Taser! This is a surprise visit. Is everything alright?"

"Yeah. I just came to scout around a little. You come up with any ideas about a home for Whiskey?"

Winston put on his serious face. "I'm afraid not. It seems the humans around here still don't have much money. I haven't peed on a new car tire in the neighborhood for a long time. Where do you suppose all their dollars went?"

I scratched behind my ear while I thought about that. "Robert says it all goes to taxes, whatever that is."

Winston knew. "Taxes are payment to the government for their work. It's how humans pay them for their job."

"Govament. I've heard of those guys, but I never figured out what their job is."

"Most of the time, they run for re-election. When they're not doing that, they argue about how to spend the taxes money."

It seemed like funny work to me. And if they were such nice guys, you'd think they'd spend some of that money on homes for dogs.

"Look—." Winston hesitated. "I hate to be blunt about this, but maybe the best way to find Whiskey a home is to have the government Animal Control people pick him up and take him to the pound. Then when humans come to find a dog to rescue, they'll take him home."

94

Winston had never been to the pound, but I had and I knew that was a bad idea. "Whiskey will never survive in there, it's filled with tough dog packs. Besides, who's gonna rescue a dog who limps? They all want the healthy young ones."

"Yes, yes, I hadn't thought about that. But even if we found a likely candidate, how will we get them to take Whiskey?"

I had a plan, it had worked for me once when I was a stray on the Westside. "It's risky, but it can work. You go sit by the human's front door and look pathetic. Then, when they open the door to come out, you whine like you need help. They feel bad and take you in."

"Sounds chancy. What if they call Animal Control on you?"

"You gotta be careful what house you go to. You hafta make sure they look nice. It's hard to tell who likes dogs, but at least you can pick the friendly humans."

Winston asked, "How do you know who's friendly?"

"There's a couple ways. If you jump on them and they don't get mad, or when they see you out walkin' around on the street, they don't ask why you're not on a leash."

"Robert doesn't know about Whiskey yet?"

"Nope. We been lucky. But we gotta do somethin' soon."

We stood and thought about that a minute, just panting.

"Is that all?" Winston asked.

That wasn't all, so I thought I'd just come out with what I thought I knew. "Winston, about the robbery, I been talkin' to Whiskey—"

Winston's eyes widened. "You're back on the case?"

"No. I was gonna say I know who it is. I know who the victim is."

"Oh." Winston head drooped a little. "I can't talk about it, Taser.

"Then tell me this much. What's Spike's master's name?"

"Louie."

"Does he have pictures on his arms?"

"Pictures? You must mean tattoos. They're called tattoos."

So then I knew I was right. Spike and his master were the victims. I figured I'd head over there and get the details straight from the dog's mouth.

THIRTEEN
Normandy, France, June 6, 1944

The brave soldiers of Able Company rode the Atlantic Channel in seven Higgins landing craft, advancing steadily toward Omaha Beach five-thousand yards away.

Second Lieutenant Peter Carter was one of thirty men from 116th Infantry huddled in the landing craft, staring at the flash of German artillery fire blasting straight at them off the distant cliff top. The artillery rounds dropped short of their boats as they continued to move closer toward D-Day invasion—and their possible death.

Peter Carter was strangely calm. He learned early in the war that the secret to keeping your fear under control was to accept the fact you were already dead. While it had helped him in battle before, today he believed it was true.

His thoughts went to Sally and the children and their life without him. She was doing her part for the war effort at home, working long hours in a ship yard. He hoped she would be all right. And his son…

Peter reached forward and slammed Kelley's helmet just ahead of him in the craft.

Kelley turned sideways, a cigarette dangling from his lips. "What!" he yelled with irritation.

"Remember what I said about Sally?"

"Yeah. I remember."

"Promise me again."

Kelley tossed his cigarette over the side. "You're crazy, Carter."

"Promise me!"

"I promise."

Peter left Kelley alone to his thoughts as they moved closer. Twenty-five hundred yards and the oncoming shells still had not found a target. In the dawning light Peter was able to see the beach clearer, but he didn't like what he saw. There were no shell holes. No cover. There was nothing from the water to the cliff but barbed wire and barricades.

Sally's face appeared, and then disappeared in the boom of distant guns.

Able Company planned to wade ashore in three files from each boat, center file first, flank files peeling right and left. Like all plans in war, luck would play a major part. Today, it seemed the luck was with the Germans. The Allied pre-invasion bombing of Omaha Beach did not hit the cliff guns. Able Company headed straight into the barrage.

What if he didn't survive the day?

Peter thought he should have just dug the coins up himself and given them to his wife. He didn't because their ownership was still illegal. Their gold value wasn't much, but it might help her someday, especially now that he knew he may not be around. But if James Kelley didn't make it home, who would tell Sally his secret? Suddenly, he felt very foolish.

Peter's boat stopped one hundred yards from the beach. His was the only Able landing craft to make it that far. At 6:36 AM the steel ramp dropped and the Germans pounded their boat with vicious machine-gun fire from their position up high. The first men out of the craft were torn by bullets, but Peter and Kelley jumped out unharmed in chest-high water and struggled toward the sand, hearts and legs pumping.

Mortar rounds exploded just ahead as machine-gun fire raked the water. When a shell exploded overhead, Peter was stunned half-conscious. He grabbed some driftwood and held on to keep from going underwater. The weight of his soggy pack pulled him down as he struggled to stay afloat. Only then did he realize the blood in the water all around him was his own.

A burst of terror filled his soul, then calm settled over him.

Faint gunfire was all he could hear.
Sally's face was all he could see.

FOURTEEN
Confronting Spike

I turned down Spike's street, still trottin'. Dogs can cover a lot of ground by trottin', and it doesn't tire me out at all like runnin. I suppose if I was a Greyhound it'd be a different story. Those crazy hounds run because it feels good, somethin' I haven't done since I was a puppy.

It does feel pretty good to run after a cat, though.

The smells were different at every house. I got a big whiff of cigarettes at the end of the street—I think the guy who lives there is a police human—and some garlic at the next house, and then some fresh paint odor from the new people remodelin'. They moved in and put all the stuff they didn't like out front.

I kept trottin'.

I admit I was pantin' a little, even though Spike's house wasn't that far from Winston's place. When I got to the side yard I went up to his gate and barked twice. He came around the corner right away, I figured he was gettin' some sun on the back patio.

Spike was old, just like his master. He was your standard Doberman, tall, with the pointy black and brown muzzle and the ears that stand straight up all the time. He was still scary lookin', even with the grey hairs on his chin.

He talked kinda funny, like he was from another country, or maybe New York.

We sniffed noses through the gate's wooden slats.

"If it ain't deputy dog," Spike said. "What brings ya over heah, Blackie?"

I let the insult slide, because I knew deep down he respected me. "Look Spike. I got this little problem and I hope you can help me out."

His eyes narrowed as they peered through the gate.

I went on. "I've got this stray dog stayin' with me, his name is Whiskey."

"Yeah? Congratulations."

"Did Winston tell you about this? The dog at my house?"

Spike shrugged. "Nah. Why should he? Am I missin' somethin' important?"

I didn't tell him right away. "Whiskey came to my back fence a few days ago. He was weak from hunger, and he had this hurt rear leg."

Spike glanced right and left, starting to look bored. "Dat right."

"I invited him to stay with me for a while to get well. After a while he told me a story about him and his master and a home robbery."

Spike's ears stood up even higher than normal.

I kept talkin'. "He told me he'd been hit with a gun bullet when his master robbed a house. That mean anything to you?"

Grrrrrrrrrrrrr.

Spike lifted a lip and snarled, then stopped.

"Look, Spike. I know he was the dog with the robber here, but it wasn't his choice. I don't want you to be mad at him."

Spike just stared at me a while, then asked. "Where's this pooch from? Westside? Or around heah?"

"I don't know. It doesn't matter, because he separated from his master. He got lost after the robbery and I don't think he's gonna see him again."

"Blackie, how come you got your nose in the middle of dis?"

"I'm just tryin' to help Whiskey. I been a stray with no home, and it's sad." I thought I'd try to get some more information out of Spike. "So tell me. Winston said the jewelry taken was very important."

"Yeah? Maybe Winston talks too much."

"He said it was a matter of life and death."

101

"Dat right," Spike said.

"Lemme tell you what happened. Whiskey's master tied the jewelry bag onto Whiskey's collar when he stopped at a store. Then he left Whiskey so long that he got out and tried to find his master. Then he got lost."

Spike pressed his nose against the gate. "Your dog's got dis bag?"

"No. That's just it. He lost it somewhere, and I tried to find it, but I ran into trouble and had to give up the search. I may know where it is, but I can't get to it because there's a bobcat in the area."

"So now youse afraid of cats?"

"This is a wildcat, he's a killer."

Spike sat down on his haunches. "Why you tellin' me all this?"

I sat down, too. "Winston said it was important. He didn't tell me it was your house that got robbed, we just figured it out."

"Who's dis we?"

"Whiskey and I. But I wanted to make sure, and I thought you should know what I know. Because if the jewelry was all that important, I wasn't gonna keep it secret."

"But you ain't lookin' for da bag no more?"

"I can't risk it. I don't want to get in a fight with a bobcat over somethin' I don't know anything about."

If I thought that might get him to talk, I was wrong.

Spike stood and backed up two steps. "Dat's a nice story, but I ain't got nothin' to add to it."

I raised a paw. "But—"

"I'll catch ya later, Blackie."

He turned and went around the corner to the back yard. I watched him disappear, surprised at his reaction and a little annoyed that was all I was gonna get out of the cranky Doberman.

I left his yard and started home. I figured if that was his attitude, I was justified in givin' up my search. If Spike didn't care, I didn't care.

I took off down the street, thinkin' about Whiskey. I figured we had a day or two, and then we were gonna try the pathetic-dog-at-the-door trick. It was time for Whiskey to leave.

Then I saw the grey Animal Control truck right in front of me.

Catcrap.

I stopped in my tracks, unsure if he'd seen me. The truck was waiting for somethin' at the end of the street. I could see an arm hangin' out the window and some guy lookin' at me in his big mirror. I didn't know what to do, so I waited. Maybe he was after coyotes or maybe the bobcat.

Then the guy opened the door and stepped out and looked straight at me. I knew who he was after. I turned around and trotted off, passing by Spike's house on the way, tryin' to stay calm. I looked over my shoulder to see if he was still there, and I didn't like what I saw. The Animal Control truck was turnin' around to come after me.

So I ran.

I ran down the street to the other corner, cutting across two yards to get away, one of them was Gizmo's. I heard him bark at me when I went by. It was gonna be close. I was three streets away from my street and the safety of my backyard. I thought I could make it but I was getting' pretty tired. My tongue was hangin out of my mouth.

I was at the corner when the Animal Control guy sped by me and slammed on his brakes a little ways ahead. He jumped out with a net on a pole and yelled at me.

HEY!

That was it. I crossed the street and started runnin' toward the park. When I chanced a look, I saw he was back in his truck and tryin' to cut me off at the park entrance. His motor roared as he tried to beat me.

I got there first and ran across the grass and straight toward the drain pipe out to the desert. I stopped just before I went through and turned to look. The Animal Control human was running toward me with his stupid pole. Just before he got there, I turned and ran down the pipe.

It was big enough for me, but not big enough for any human to go through.

HEY YOU!

I made to the other side but kept runnin' out toward the wash. If he decided to hop the fence, I didn't want to be around. I jumped down in the wash and hid behind a big creosote bush. I stood there, breathin' hard, catchin' my breath, then I snuck a look at the park. He was waiting in the park for me.

Let him wait, I wasn't going anywhere.

I panted and thought of my next move. All of a sudden I picked up an evil smell. At first I wasn't sure, but the scent was too strong. Then I saw bobcat tracks in the sand. He was very close by. I had to go back before the wildcat picked up my scent. I had to get out of the desert.

But I couldn't.

FIFTEEN
Baltimore, Maryland August, 1945

Sally Carter packed her last blouse in her suitcase and took a final look around her small apartment. The sagging couch and the lumpy beds did not belong to her, so they would stay but not be missed. The only item she owned was her Singer sewing machine, and she planned to leave it in exchange for some back rent. Her landlord had been gracious about it. Part of his war effort, he said.

Everyone was used to sacrificing during the war. The unknown now was what life would be like after the war. She couldn't help thinking things would get better. Certainly Peter's death benefit would help, but her widow's pension would only go so far.

She sat and waited, tuning her Crosley radio while she waited for Tommy to get home from Karsten's with his snacks for the train.

So when the knock on the door came, she opened it, expecting to see her son. What she saw brought her hand to her mouth. For one hopeful second, she believed the handsome soldier standing in front of her was her husband.

"Oh," was all she could say. Her face fell when she realized the truth.

"Sally Carter?" the soldier asked.

"I am."

He was tall like Peter, with kind eyes. "I'm James Kelley. I served with your husband in Able Company."

She just stared at him and his uniform, her emotions racing.

"May I come in?" he asked.

Sally opened the door wide. "Yes, I'm sorry."

He followed her into the room and took an offered seat on the couch. She noticed his limp, but said nothing, and for a moment, neither did he. Glen Miller played on in their awkward silence.

Sally was curious about the visit but afraid to ask. She didn't sit, but motioned toward the tiny kitchen. "Would you like a glass of water?"

"Yes, please."

She filled a glass and returned to the couch. He took the water in hand but just stared at it

"Have you come a long way?" she asked.

"New York." He glanced around the apartment. "I gather you've been working in the shipyards? For Bethlehem?"

She nodded. "A scaler, on Liberty ships. It's difficult work, but not as hard as being a waitress. Certainly the pay is better." She paused. "Or it was."

Kelley took a drink and then stared out the window. "My sister was a welder. Small stuff. You know, decking plates, stairs."

"I knew a few welders. They're back home knitting now. It's funny…" Her voice trailed off.

Then he said it. "Peter. We were at Omaha together. He died bravely."

Sally nodded in appreciation, but she had never doubted that.

He continued. "We all knew it could be bad, we didn't know how bad. We just knew it was necessary. But Peter asked me to come see you if he didn't make it. I'm sorry it took so long, I was recuperating. The hospital only released me three weeks ago."

"I'm sorry." Sally wrung her hands, thinking only of her husband and that fateful day.

"I have a message from Peter. He wanted you to know how much he loved you and Tommy."

She nodded numbly.

"But there was something else."

She looked in his eyes, but was afraid to ask what.

106

"He had some coins hidden, some twenty-dollar gold pieces he was convinced would be worth a lot someday. He wanted to make sure you got them."

"Coins?" Sally hesitated. "He never said anything about coins."

"He didn't want to get you in trouble for hoarding gold. He thought the government would take them, or they might be stolen from you."

This was totally unexpected. "What are they worth? Do you know how many?"

Kelley thought. "About two dozen. He said he had one for each year minted. It should be a little over a thousand dollars."

She sat in stunned surprise. One thousand dollars was an unbelievable windfall.

"He said when he started it was just about coin collecting, but then he grew to think the gold value would rise.

"Where are these coins?" Sally asked

"They're buried in his grandparent's back yard in Chester Springs. Are your in-laws still there?"

"Yes, it's their house now. Grandpa has passed and they take care of grandma. Why didn't he tell me about this?"

"He thought the government would take them from you, or they might be stolen. He didn't want to put you in danger."

"How can I find them? They have a very large backyard, I wouldn't know where to start looking."

"They're buried ten paces west of the old oak tree. But he thought you should leave them in the ground as long as possible."

Sally fingered her frayed cotton dress. Extra money after all the lean years would be a Godsend. But she had Peter's death benefit put away in savings, and she had her war widow's pension, so she thought she could honor his wish. She could wait.

Kelley glanced at her packed suitcases and set his glass down. "Do you have a place to go?"

"Yes. Tommy and I are going to live with my parents until we get settled. They aren't that far from Chester Springs. The family will help."

"Of course. Can I help you get to the station?"

"That won't be necessary, I have a taxi coming. I'm just waiting for Tommy. He had to get some jawbreakers."

Kelley adjusted at his bad leg, then stood. "I should get back, my wife…"

"Of course. Well, I can't thank you enough."

"Remember. Ten paces west of the old oak." He held her hand for a moment. "Peter was a good man. It's wonderful he left you something valuable."

A good man. She closed the door as he left, thinking. Yes. *More than you know.*

SIXTEEN
Labs with a Plan

I waited as long as I could, but I had to move, it wasn't safe where I was hiding. I popped up out of the sandwash and cut through the open desert, heading toward the backside of my house. I knew the Animal Control guy would see me, but if I stayed in the wash I might get ambushed by the bobcat.

I hustled through the sage and the bristlebrush on a faint trail I'd been down before. It was only a couple houses to Robert's.

When I got there, I turned around and looked for predators. The only one I thought was around was at the park with a catch pole.

I barked at Whiskey. "Hey!"

He poked his nose out and saw it was me.

I called again. "Whiskey! Come here."

He hobbled up to the metal bars of the fence separating our backyard from the desert. "What're you doing out there?"

"It's a long story and I don't have time to talk. Go in the house and get Meatloaf, I need to talk to him quick."

Whiskey didn't say a word, he turned around and hustled to the dog door. I took another nervous look around. I didn't mind fighting a coyote, but I was no match for these wildcats. They got teeth *and* claws, and the claws can do some real damage. I got swiped across the nose by a house cat once, but this was more serious.

It took a minute before Meatloaf appeared with a sleepy look on his face. He yawned on his way over to talk to me.

I waited impatiently. "Meat. I need your help."

"What's up?"

109

"The Animal Control guy is after me, he's down at the park and he's blockin' my way home. He's got his truck and his pole and he's mad."

"Catcrap." Meatloaf looked concerned. "Dog, you don't want to go back to the pound. You got enemies there."

He didn't need to tell me that.

Meatloaf looked at our view fence stretching all the way across the back yard. It was as tall as Robert. "Too bad you can't jump like Gizmo."

I wasn't built like a Jack Russell. We had to do it the fat Labrador way. "The side gate is still open," I told him. "I need you to draw the dogcatcher guy away from the park."

Meatloaf looked confused. "How can I do that?"

"We look like each other, we can fool the guy."

"But I'm fatter than you."

"Just run down there and let him see you. He'll think it's me and he'll chase you down the street."

"Oh great, what could go wrong with that idea?"

"I admit, it's flawed."

"Dog, you're stressin' me out."

"Meat. Listen to me. I'm worried about the bobcat roamin' around out here. I saw his tracks in the wash and I can smell him as well as I can smell you."

"Alright, but I got a bad feeling about this."

"It will be fine, just don't let him get too close to you. Draw him toward Gizmo's house, then cross the street and run home once he starts to move away. I'll be watchin' from the desert and scoot by when he's gone. We should hit the backyard about the same time."

"What if he follows us home?"

"He can't do anything once we're in the yard. We're legal then."

"I got a bad feeling about this."

"Meat. You want me to get killed by a bobcat? Or get thrown in the pound?"

He turned around and looked at Whiskey lifting his leg on a bush. "This is all the stray dog's fault."

"Don't blame Whiskey, he can't help it. Besides, it's really my fault, I invited him to stay here."

Meatloaf sighed. "Taser, normal Labradors like eating and sleeping. You hafta investigate. You sure there's no German Shepherd in you?"

"Dunno. You can do this, can't you?"

"I guess. But if I end up in the pound you gotta come get me."

"He won't catch you. Just give me a little time to get down to the park so I can sneak by once he gets in his truck and drives after you."

"Ok. But I got a bad—"

I took off for the park before he finished complaining. But I had a nagging thought this wasn't my best plan.

***

Meatloaf watched Taser leave and then tried to remember how long it took to get to the park. He waited that long, then a little longer. Truth was, he wasn't too smart about time. All he knew was there was an awful lot of it between first meal and second meal.

Meatloaf looked at Whiskey. "Hey. You better hide. We may be getting visitors soon."

Whiskey didn't say anything but went in his dog house.

Meatloaf went to the side gate and stuck his head out. It was a little hard to see all the way to the park, but he could see one of those grey boxy trucks they used to put animals in. Taser was right. The govament was after them.

He sighed, but then went right out to the sidewalk and walked slowly down toward the truck.

There was one house left to walk by before he got to the park and he still didn't see the dogcatcher. It didn't look like anyone was sitting in the truck, but he couldn't see anyone in the park. Meatloaf walked closer.

Yeah. Over there.

The dogcatcher was in the park hiding next to a bush. Meatloaf took a deep breath and walked right to the entrance of the park. He stood there waiting but the guy didn't see him, he was looking out in the desert.

Hey stupid, here I am.

This human didn't seem to be a very good dogcatcher, Meatloaf thought. So he barked to get his attention.

WOOF!

Oh oh.

The guy started running flat out toward Meatloaf, so he turned and ran. Meatloaf ran down the street away from his house, away from the park, away from the crazy human chasing him. He got to the end of the block before he chanced a look back.

The guy was in his truck and moving. Meatloaf ran down Gizmo's street, his heart pumping and his breathing labored. Maybe he shouldn't have drunk so much water. He was in no shape for this, he was a house dog.

Stupid Taser.

Once he got around the corner he ran across the grass yard to the front porch of Gizmo's house and lay down by the front door. He hid behind a planter and kept his head down, panting like a puppy chasing a ball.

He heard the Animal Control truck driving slowly down the street. Then Gizmo started barking inside the house.

Ruff Ruff Ruff

Great.

The truck slowed in front of the house, creeping along like he was stalking victims. Gizmo kept barking. Meatloaf hugged the concrete and closed his eyes, remembering how nice and calm his life was when he lived in Fresno. No stress. Plenty of food. No crazy roommate.

The grey truck stopped in front of Gizmo's house and sat with the motor running. Meatloaf opened his eyes and peered through the flowers in the planter. The dog catcher was still in his truck, but Gizmo wouldn't shut up.

Ruff Ruff Ruff, Ruff Ruff Ruff, Ruff Ruff Ruff

Finally the truck pulled away and drove slowly down the street. Meatloaf got up and watched him leave. Now all he had to do was go the other way back to the street corner, and then get past the park to his house. He was tempted to say something to Gizmo but he resisted, he could explain later. Right now he had to let some of that time pass so Taser could get through the park and get home. So he waited.

He waited until the truck drove out of sight before he moved. Even so, Meatloaf stayed close to the houses on the street, hugging the bushes planted along the front.

He made it to the corner with no problem and trotted on the sidewalk toward the park. When he got to the park he looked for Taser but didn't see him. He figured his buddy must be home, so Meatloaf relaxed.

He paused at the park to pee on his favorite bush, thinking how those govament guys were no match for crafty Labradors. Labradors may be fat but they aren't stupid. But as he turned to leave for home, he saw the grey truck turning down the street coming straight toward him.

Catcrap.

If Meatloaf tried to get to his home he would run right into the dogcatcher.

So he ran up to the closest house and hugged the front. When he saw the house garage door was open, he ran inside and lay down behind the car parked close to one wall. He saw the grey govament truck drive slowly by and stop at the park. The dogcatcher got out, but it seemed he was looking at the park, not in the garage where he was hiding.

Meatloaf waited. More time passed. Time that he knew could be better spent sleeping on his living room rug.

But no.

Finally he heard the motor of the grey govament truck start. But he also heard the door to the house open. Then he saw an arm and hand appear to hit the garage door button. The big door shut tight, trapping the scared Lab hiding behind the car.

Great.

Now what?

It was dark in the garage, and he didn't even know where he was. He thought about barking for a minute, but didn't want the dog catcher to hear him. He used his nose to search for clues about his predicament.

Meatloaf's nose twitched happily at the smell of food. It wasn't a food he was familiar with or had ever eaten. He wasn't even sure if it qualified for food, because Labradors had a problem distinguishing what was food and what was simply edible.

Simply edible worked fine for Meatloaf.

Besides, since he was locked up, he thought he may miss second meal, so why not eat? He got up from behind the car and walked closer to the door where boxes and bags were set out. He sniffed each one until he found the source of the smell. It wasn't open, but he knew what it was anyway and it turned his stomach.

Cat food.

It wasn't the box of food that upset Meatloaf's stomach, it was the realization he was trapped in old man Crenshaw's garage.

SEVENTEEN
Taser, out in the Desert

Once I got close to the park I hid behind a bush. I could see the grey truck but I couldn't see the dogcatcher. I knew he must be in the park waiting for me to come home. He was waiting for me to come through the pipe so he could grab me and drag me off to the pound.

Old man Crenshaw must have called the Animal Control people and told them about my roamin' the neighborhood. At times like this, I almost wished I was back livin' on the Westside. They're not so uptight about stray dogs wanderin' the streets over there.

I thought Meatloaf shoulda been there, it seemed too much time had passed. I was jumpy because I could still smell the bobcat. I raised my head and took another look, but nothin' was happening.

No. I was wrong.

Something was happening, and it wasn't good. I got a strong scent of bobcat, a bobcat that was very close. I got up and moved away from the park, walking quickly further out in the desert.

The smell was close by, probably in the sandwash. The bobcat was probably out on a hunt along his normal trail. I'd seen his prints and picked up his scent, there was no mistaking it.

I wasn't sure what to do. If I got too far away from the park I wouldn't be able to escape. If I went too far out I could get trapped by the bobcat and have to fight my way out. At that moment all I wanted to do was get away. I wasn't sure if he'd picked up my scent or if he was even interested, but I wasn't stickin' around.

The trail I was on kept goin' past our subdivision, so I left it and walked among the leafy brush and desert trees. The old Mesquites were bent over and hugging the desert floor, not trimmed up like the desert trees in my yard. These low-hanging branches made a good spot for hiding places, so I was careful and I stayed away from them. The brush was thick off the trail, sharp branches raked my coat as I squeezed between the bushes.

The bobcat scent was strong now. I thought he was followin' me along the wash. I had to find another way out of there, but I was trapped with the subdivision fence on one side and the sandwash on the other. I couldn't get over the fence and couldn't risk crossing the wash.

This thing probably blended into the desert, it was his home. I couldn't see him but I knew he was there because his scent was intense. I looked right and left, then behind me. I was spooked by this thing, I didn't know how to fight and win. Cats were too quick. I had to make a choice between bobcat or dog pound.

I'd take my chances with the dog catcher.

I turned away from the open desert and headed back to the safety of the fence line. I'd follow it back to the park and the drainage pipe and take my chances gettin' home.

If only Meatloaf would get there and do his job

***

When the bobcat first smelled the dog it crouched low, his tail flicking gently, his nose sampling the scent. A dog had invaded his territory, and the cat was immediately wary. A dog was a formidable foe, but not unbeatable. Dogs were loud and full of themselves, but slow and slow-witted. A few breeds were dangerous, but most were no match for this hunter.

Still, the wildcat was cautious. It was not normal for one of these animals to enter his hunting ground. He'd only seen dogs in their homes, barking in warning but sheltered from risk.

One small dog had been tethered by a chain in its backyard, he had killed it easily. But a canine roaming free was to be respected if not

116

feared. He sampled the air again. This dog especially deserved respect. The bobcat did not smell fear or victim.

Still, in these surroundings, the cat knew he had the advantage. He was hungry and he was a hunter. It was his nature to kill and he would kill today.

He rose and moved when the dog moved, but staying in the shelter of the sandwash. The sides of the wash and the desert brush afforded concealment and stealth. The dog did not seem to be aware he was being hunted. If he did know, he was not afraid.

The dog moved away from the park. The bobcat followed, staying hidden in the wash. The dog was coming closer now, closer to the wash. The wildcat crouched. He would let this prey come to him.

His claws sheathed and unsheathed, anticipating an attack. His leg muscles tensed as the dog came closer to the wash. He would wait, then rush and pounce and slash, relying on speed and surprise.

The dog came closer—then stopped.

He stopped just out of distance, paused, then turned and moved quickly toward the human houses and then toward the park again. The bobcat followed, staying in the wash just behind the dog, who was moving faster now.

The bobcat knew he must be quicker. He ran ahead of the dog, them jumped out of the wash and cut across the desert. He would catch the dog just at the park where their paths merged. The bobcat wanted his prey to stumble into his attack so the element of surprise was his.

When he reached a cluster of bush on the trail he stopped and hugged the desert floor. Just then he heard a different dog bark once at the entrance of the park, but he was only interested in the canine coming toward him.

He waited to pounce.

***

I was very close to the park when I heard my buddy's bark.

WOOF!

Finally Meatloaf had come to draw away the dogcatcher. Now I could get through the park safely without some idiot govament guy chasin' me. I saw him come out from behind a bush and run toward his truck. When I heard it start and drive away, I trotted toward the pipe into the park. I only had a few minutes before he might come back, I wanted to get home.

I was thinking how difficult this simple trip to visit Spike had become—when suddenly everything changed. I froze in my tracks, my senses on high alert, my nose full of a strong scent of bobcat. The hair on my back rose as I crouched slightly.

I peered through the dense brush, sampling the air for hints on his location. There was no doubt what this bobcat was doing.

He was coming to kill me.

EIGHTEEN
New Brunswick, New Jersey 1975

Thomas Carter ducked into Tumulty's Pub and took a seat at the bar. He set his briefcase down and put his elbows on the polished bar top. Matthew, the owner, recognized him and drew a Guinness from the tap. He set it on the bar.

"You're late," he joked.

"Semester finals," Thomas said as he took a sip. "My students come first."

Matthew polished a glass. "You hear about Hoffa?"

"Yeah. Wadda you think?"

"He swims with the fishes."

"Mafia?" Thomas asked.

"Gotta be, you don't piss off those boys. They'll never find that body, trust me. He's at the bottom of some landfill."

"Good riddance," Matthew said.

"Not a Teamster fan?"

"Just jealous of their pay, this inflation is killing me. Last fillup I paid sixty cents for premium."

Thomas smiled. "You tellin' me you gotta sell the Cadillac?"

Matthew took the dig in stride. "If Rutgers paid you what you're worth, you'd have some decent transportation, too."

"Carol wants a house, not a new car"

"I'd listen to her," Matthew said. "A house may turn out to be your best inflation hedge."

Thomas sighed. "I can't seem to get the money together for twenty percent down. Every time we get close, prices jump out of reach.

You're talking forty thousand now for a three bedroom. And the interest rates…"

Matthew walked away to draw a beer for another customer, then returned. "What about those coins your mom left you?"

Thomas pulled on his Guinness and set it down on a napkin. "Coins, yeah. I haven't looked at those in years."

"Gold's legal now, right?"

"Since January. A parting gift from Tricky Dick."

Matthew snorted. "Good riddance to him, too."

"Too bad he's not with Hoffa."

"Why not sell 'em?"

"The coins? I don't know about that, my dad left us those. There's a lot of sentimental value there. They've been in the family for decades."

"You wouldn't have to sell them all."

Thomas tipped his near empty glass. "That's true."

"I'd consider it if I was you. Gold's close to two hundred now."

Thomas calculated quickly in his head. "Damn. With our savings that would do it."

Matthew wiped the bar and put down a dry napkin. "A wife deserves her own place."

That was true.

Forty-five minutes later, Thomas Carter stood on a kitchen chair with screwdriver in hand, removing two screws holding on the heater register in their small apartment. He pocketed the screws, set the metal register on the floor and reached deep inside the vent. He felt around until he found the wrapped and padded box holding his coins.

Thomas took it to the kitchen table, opened it carefully and looked inside. Every time he saw them, he was amazed at how the gold coins never lost their luster, even after all the years. He dug them out and placed them on the table in shiny rows, arranged carefully year by year.

1907, 1908, 1909…all the way to 1933.

There was one coin for each year, except for the years of World War One when none were minted. It was a fine collection, but now they had a job to do. He would sell the coins so they could buy their first house.

But not all of the coins. He would keep one as a remembrance of his father, a father he could barely picture.

Thomas picked up the 1907 Saint Gaudens twenty-dollar gold piece and held it close, feeling its weight, considering. That was the first year they were made, that should mean something to a collector. The coin was worn but still shiny. Unsure which would be best to keep, he set the 1907 down and picked up the 1933. It still looked brand new. Maybe that was the better choice.

Thomas went through the kitchen drawers until he found a small leather pouch, then he placed the 1933 coin inside. He stuck it in the bottom of his sock drawer, and then put the rest of the coins back in their box.

He debated waiting until Carol got home, but he feared the dealers would be closed by then. Besides, he wanted to surprise her.

He flipped through the yellow pages in search of a coin dealer, surprised by how many were listed. He chose the closest one on Neilson Street and dialed their number to find out how late they were open. Six pm. There was just enough time.

Thomas got in his '62 Volkswagen with his box of coins and a smile on his face. It was the right decision. He felt even his father would approve. Some day they may help you out of a jam, his mother had said.

It was ten to six when Thomas entered Atlantic Gold and Silver. The store was empty except for grey-haired gentleman, slightly stooped with age. Thomas set his box on the counter and introduced himself.

Store owner George Conway shook his hand. "Maybe we should go in my office. Let me lock the door."

George turned the key and led Thomas to the rear of the store. A huge black safe and a sagging wooden desk left little room in the messy office. Thomas stood holding his box while Fred cleared papers and books to find a clean space on the top.

121

"Let's see what you have," he said

Thomas set the coins on the desk. George picked one up at a time and examined it carefully. Finally he spoke.

"Quite a collection. And they're in remarkable shape."

Thomas shrugged. "My dad was the collector, not me. He believed they would go up in value."

"They have. If I may ask, why are you selling these? If you hold on to them a little longer, they will surely go up more."

"My wife and I are trying to get together the down payment on a house."

"I see. This should certainly do it. Unless you're buying the Mayor's house." He glanced down at the coins again, then looked up. "Is this all the Saint Gaudens you have?"

Thomas hesitated, then nodded.

"You're missing the 1933, the last year they were minted. That coin would complete the collection."

"I know. Does that mean you don't want to buy these years?"

"No, no. I want them. But…" Fred looked at him closely. "If you had the 1933 I would be very interested in buying it."

Thomas was quiet, then he had to ask. "Why that one?"

Fred shrugged. "It's very rare, not many got in circulation before they were recalled. In fact, I don't know of any left anywhere. That damn Roosevelt melted them all down."

"I see." For a moment Thomas thought of the money, then the blurred memory of a tall man bending down to hug him came to mind.

"No," he said. "This is all I have to sell."

NINETEEN
Labs in Trouble

Meatloaf returned to his hiding spot behind the car in the garage and lay down to think. Thinking was always painful for him, but once he got down to it, he was surprised by what he came up with.

Meatloaf wanted to get out of there and go home, it was cold and dark inside. For a moment he thought the solution was to bark until Crenshaw opened the door. But he worried Crenshaw might leave him in there and call the Animal Control.

Maybe he would wait until the old guy opened the door to drive to the store or the doctor or wherever old people drive. But Crenshaw was retired, so it might be days before he drove anywhere.

He shuddered at the thought, he'd been trapped in the garage before and it was awful. It happened one time in Fresno when his master smoked so much marijuana he forgot where he'd put his dog. Meatloaf was in there the whole weekend. Now it was happening to him again.

He could be trapped in Crenshaw's for two days!

Meatloaf thought about what he might miss while imprisoned for two days. There were two meals a day for two days...that's...that's seven meals, plus the one he wouldn't get that night...that's...that's eleven meals! That's too many, he'd be dead in two days.

Meatloaf sighed. He always knew someday he would die of hunger.

He was gonna die in this stinkin' garage because of some stupid stray dog Taser brought home. Taser. What kind of Labrador brings home stray dogs? See what all that compassion gets you?

He could use some of that compassion about now. Maybe Taser and Gizmo would come looking for him. Maybe Robert would. Maybe he'd starve so thin he could slide under the garage door.

123

Or maybe he could sustain himself with some of that cat food.

Meatloaf rose and walked over to the box and sniffed it again. It was definitely cat food, it smelled fishy and disgusting. Oh well. He'd eaten worse things.

Meatloaf grabbed the unopened box up with his teeth and carried it behind the car. He lay with it between his front paws and gnawed on the cardboard until he'd made a little hole in the side, then a big hole. The smelly nuggets spilled out on the concrete floor

He tried eating a few of them. Ehhh. It wasn't bad for a snack, but certainly not worth eating everyday. No matter, it was better than dying of hunger. He kept munching. The stuff was growing on him.

Suddenly he remembered the whole reason for this adventure, helping his buddy escape through the park. He wondered if Taser had made it home alright.

***

As soon as I saw him I took a step backward. The bobcat had to be just ahead, blocking my only way out of the desert. I was trapped and it shocked me, then angered me. I switched my thinking from losing to winning. This bobcat wasn't going to get me today.

I didn't have time to think, I just reacted. I got off the trail and moved away from him, moved closer to the park. I didn't want to make it easy for him. When I got there, I stopped and turned, hoping to get a look at the wildcat. I couldn't spot him through the brush, so the advantage was all his.

Then I saw him.

The bobcat was spotted and striped in colors that blended right into the desert. His head was small but his muscular body looked like a compact mountain lion. He was more enemy than I bargained for.

He stood just off the trail, head hanging low, cold eyes staring at me with no trace of fear. I knew I was out of my element here. I was simply prey to this hunter, and hunting was his natural state. He killed for food. I begged for food.

My bite wouldn't be much of a weapon against four legs tipped with claws. Not to mention the cat's razor sharp teeth. Even if I got him by the throat he could claw me bloody. I had to use my brain. I had to use common sense. There was only one thing to do.

Run like a scalded dog

I looked. He wasn't moving yet, but his legs were flexed like he was ready to jump. I was a little closer to the pipe than he was, but I thought he would beat me to the exit. My only chance was to fool him.

I took off running straight at him. He tensed but didn't move. When I was halfway there I jumped off the trail and ran flat out for the drain pipe. Out of the corner of my eye I saw him start after me, his body stretching and gathering as he ran. He was fast!

I dodged the large creosote and jumped over the small brush. I couldn't look but I knew he was right behind me. I was almost there but so was he. It was gonna be close.

When I got to the opening I barely slowed, just ducked and started in, but then—

***

Meatloaf had eaten half the box of cat food when he was hit with a serious intestinal cramp. Maybe cat food didn't agree with his stomach after all. He got up and walked around the garage to find a place to poop.

In the near dark he could see piles of newspapers and big boxes against one wall and an old bicycle leaning against the other. That left the open space next to the car. He reconsidered, thinking maybe this was a bad idea. Maybe he should try to hold it.

Or maybe, Meatloaf thought, this was his way out.

He knew humans hated the smell of dog poop. He'd seen that his whole life. So if he pooped in the garage and Crenshaw came out and

125

smelled it, he'd open the big door to get rid of the smell. Then Meatloaf could slip out unseen.

Brilliant.

Meatloaf picked the biggest open area on the garage floor, then walked in a tight circle until he got pointed in the preferred direction, then he left his business.

Feeling much better, he ran back behind the car and waited. He figured any minute Crenshaw would come to check on the smell. But then he remembered how bad human noses were. They probably couldn't smell the poop with the house door closed. Meatloaf gave it a little more time.

When nothing happened, he thought he better make some noise so the old guy would come out.

WOOF

One bark should do it.

Nothing happened.

Maybe two barks.

WOOF WOOF

The door to the house opened and the overhead light came on.

What the hell…

The door slammed shut, then opened again. Old man Crenshaw stuck his head out and looked around, muttering.

What the hell is that?

He fumbled with the button next to the door as the big garage door jumped and banged and started to roll up. Meatloaf waited impatiently at his spot behind the car. When the door was open head-high he slipped out and took off for home, leaving Crenshaw looking at the poop and scratching his head.

By the time he walked outside to look up and down the street, Meatloaf was safely in his backyard.

***

The bobcat and I reached the pipe at the same time. I scooted in but he stopped dead. But I didn't get away clean. Just as I entered the tunnel, the cat swiped hard with his paw.

OWW!

He raked my rear haunch with his claws. The force of the blow bounced me into the side of the pipe, but I kept runnin'. I was as scared as I've ever been in my life.

When I popped out in the park I didn't look back. I ran to my street and halfway home. When I finally turned around to look, the bobcat was gone. I figured he wouldn't follow me into the subdivision and I was right.

The slash on my rear hip hurt bad enough to tell me I was lucky to get away. Any fight between me and him would have gone badly. For the rest of the way I settled down to a walk. The wound didn't bother me too much, I'd been hurt worse. At least it wasn't a gun bullet wound like Whiskey had.

Our house looked especially friendly. I slipped through the open gate and went to the backyard.

Whiskey popped out of his house when he saw me. "Taser, you're bleeding. What happened?"

I turned around and looked at my haunch. "Yeah. Cat trouble."

It was cut but not very bad. It wasn't my first wound, Robert had bandaged me before. "I was right about that bobcat. You don't want to mess around with him."

"Don't worry," Whiskey said. "I'm not looking for trouble. In fact, I don't want to trouble you much longer. I think I should be leaving soon."

This shocked me. "But Whiskey, where will you go?"

He looked at his paws. "I don't know. But I can walk better now, I have a limp, that's all. I'll show you."

Whiskey hobbled around the back patio, limping badly on his wounded leg. He didn't look in good enough shape to walk very far. Certainly not yet.

"The leg looks better, but don't leave just yet, the pack is workin' on finding you a home."

"Really?"

"Stay here a little longer. Please."

"Ok, thanks Taser. Thanks a lot"

I didn't tell him things looked bad for finding him a home. I didn't want to give up hope myself. But right then I was tired and needed sleep. And I was curious about my buddy.

"Is Meatloaf back yet?" I asked.

"He came in a little bit ago. He went right in the house."

"Thanks, I better check on him."

I walked slowly to the dog door and went inside to find my buddy. He was just where I thought he might be, sprawled out on the living room rug.

He lifted his head when I came over. "Hey Taser."

"How'd it go?" I asked.

"No problem," he said. "You?" He looked at my rear and then sniffed. "That smells like blood on your butt."

"The bobcat took a swipe at me. Nothin' a bandage won't fix. I'll tell you about it after dinner."

At that we both lay down and took a long nap. We were still snorin' when Robert walked in the front door.

TWENTY
Regroup at the Park

Before dinner, Robert washed my wound with soap and water, then went ahead and gave me a whole bath out on the driveway. It was cold, but when he finished toweling me off I felt great. Only then I realized I was starvin'. When the chow hit the dish, I beat Meatloaf to the bottom of the bowl.

I had to sit through a little lecture Robert gave me when he saw my bleeding haunch, but I don't think he had any idea how I got it. Maybe he thought I'd run into the fence chasin' Meatloaf, something I'd done once before. If he really knew what I did, he would have given me a bigger lecture. So I sat on my butt with a serious look on my face and listened as he pointed his finger at me and talked. I love Robert, but I didn't pay attention to what he said. I've heard it before. Besides, humans don't know everything.

After that, he went to the cabinet and got this tube of gushy stuff and put some on my wound. It felt a lot better after that. He didn't put a bandage on it, so I figured the cut must not have been too deep.

Then we had to wait while he made dinner. I was worried we might be late to the park, and I hate that. Half the fun is smellin' other dogs, and I didn't want to miss anyone's butt.

Robert took something from the cold box and put it in the little oven in the cabinet. Then he watched it turn in circles like me and Meatloaf do to find the right spot to lie down. Finally, a bell rang and he opened the door. When he put it in it there it didn't smell like anything, but when he took it out it smelled great. Meatloaf said it was pot roast, whatever that is. Didn't matter, we didn't get any, no matter how hard we stared.

129

At least we didn't hafta wait for him to do the dishes 'cause Robert used cardboard plates. Finally he went to the drawer with our leashes and hooked us up—for Mister Crenshaw's benefit—and then we were off to the park.

I looked for Simba but she wasn't there yet. I didn't want her to think I was ignoring her, but I suppose I was. With Whiskey and Spike and the bobcat, I'd been busy. I was probably in trouble with her. She's a high-maintenance hound, so she probably wouldn't understand. I can't help that. Sometimes, a Lab's gotta do what a Lab's gotta do.

It was only when we got to the park that I heard all about Meatloaf's adventure getting' trapped in Crenshaw's garage. He told Gizmo and Roxie all about it. Remi was there too, but he didn't seem to like the story.

Remi finally interrupted us. "I'll have you know, I don't find this tale amusing. After you two Afghans were through with him, that Animal Control person came down my street. I was out in my yard minding my own business, and…"

"Since when?" interrupted Roxie.

Remi looked at her. "I beg your pardon?"

Roxie let him have it. "Since when do you mind your own business? You're always criticizing us dogs for what we do."

Remi sniffed. "Someone has to uphold minimal community standards around here. I guess it falls on me." He cleared his throat. "As I was saying, this Animal Control person observed me lounging in my own yard and came to our front door. He instructed my master that all dogs are required to be on a leash outside of the home. Even me."

"So what?" I said. "That's been the rule around here for years."

"But enforcement was not strict before you started running around upsetting everyone, including Mister Crenshaw."

"Old man Crenshaw's just crabby," Meatloaf said. "What's his problem, anyway?"

Winston appeared out of nowhere with the answer. "I heard his wife died of cancer a few months ago. The poor bloke is still upset."

"He's probably lonely," said Roxie. "He must miss his mate."

Remi didn't seem to care. "Whatever his problem may be, Taser and Meatloaf are making things worse. Now I can't even go out in my own front yard."

"I feel for you, Remi, but there's more important stuff happenin' around here," I said.

"Like what?" Gizmo asked.

"None of us will be safe until we run this bobcat out of our neighborhood. It won't be long until he's walkin' our streets lookin' for victims, just like the coyotes."

Meatloaf explained my concern. "Taser tangled with the bobcat today. Just outside the park."

Remi inspected my butt and smirked. "It looks like the bobcat won."

I ignored the fuzzy creep. "Dog's are no match for this thing. Not even Harley could take this killer."

"Oh no," Roxie disagreed. "I bet Harley could."

Winston raised a paw. "If he's such a tough bugger, how come he's only doffed Crenshaw's cat. It seems like small potatoes for a vicious blagger."

"He's taking the easy prey first. If he gets away with that, he'll keep coming back."

Gizmo looked confused. "How can we get rid of a bobcat if we can't win a fight with it?"

"I gotta admit," I said. "Right now I don't know. Lemme think about it."

"Oh great," Remi said. "I presume we should anticipate more trouble."

"Shut up, Remi. You'd be the first to bark for help if this bobcat jumped into your back yard."

Just then Harley the Rottweiler showed up

Roxie beamed. "Good thing you showed up, Harley. They're talkin' trash about you."

"Wassa problem?" Harley said.

I explained. "We're talkin' about how tough the bobcat is. I know you're tough, but…"

"That's right, Jack. I'm black and bad."

Harley was mostly black and he certainly looked mean. He had a head as big as a bowling ball. I figure he was a hundred and twenty pounds of muscle. Still, this cat was armed with more than teeth.

"Dog, this things got more claws than you got hairs on your head. Look at my rear." I turned to show him.

"Ouch. Look Jack, thas bad, but I ain't afraid a no cat, big or little. I'll bite his head off."

"Good plan. But don't start the fight, it ain't worth it."

Then I brought up my other problem. "Has anyone found a likely home for Whiskey?"

"Whynchew keep him?" Harley asked. "He don't cause no problem. Most days I don't even know he's there."

I looked at Meatloaf. "I don't think Robert will take a third dog. We make enough mess for three dogs now."

Meatloaf looked nervous. "Now hang on a minute. There's not enough food to go around our house now."

Harley snorted. "You look like you doin' alright."

"My weight is not your problem," Meatloaf said. "I happen to need more nutrition than your average dog."

I looked at Gizmo. "Hey Giz. Didn't you say somethin' about your neighbor?"

Gizmo nodded. "I talked to the Weimaraner across the street from me. He said last week that his masters wanted another dog. But yesterday he said now they can't afford it. Something about taxes going up. What's taxes?"

"It's money that humans pay to the govament so they can hire more dogcatchers."

132

"I don't like taxes," said Meatloaf.

"Nobody does."

"So why have them?"

"The govament needs money."

"Why doesn't the govament get its money by working at a job?"

"They don't have to. They get free taxes."

Remi objected. "Dogs don't work and we get free food."

"We earn it. We get food because we're cute," Roxie said.

"They shouldn't take money from dog homes," I said. "I don't think we need all those dogcatchers."

"We need dogcatchers to keep order," Remi said. "That costs money."

"It doesn't seem right."

"Taxes are not about what's right, they're about what's fair."

It didn't seem fair to me either. I left the discussion to them and ran out in the park. I stopped runnin' because my rear leg started hurtin'. I settled on sniffin' bushes. I got some great dog pee smells because the sprinklers were on earlier and made everything kinda wet. I was so intent on dog stuff I almost forgot about my problems, but then Winston brought them back to me.

He waddled up to talk. "Taser. I need to speak to you privately."

"Yeah? What's up?"

"There's been a new development." Winston looked around to see if anyone was listening. He lowered his already deep voice and stepped closer. "I have an urgent message from Spike. He needs you to bob on over so he can bend your ear."

I cocked my head. "What?"

Winston paused, then said. "He needs to talk to you."

"Why didn't you say so?"

"Sorry. A bit of British slang."

"You're British?"

"Quite."

"I thought you were an English Bulldog. From the country of England."

"I am. Britain, England—same cup of tea."

I tried to get my canine brain around that, but I couldn't. Things like counting and measuring and time were strange to me. I knew where I lived and the area around it, but anything else was just out of my world. "I don't know much about geometry. Is England near New York?"

"Just across the pond. Why do you ask?"

"It seems like everything revolves around New York. Is that true?"

"Only to New Yorkers."

That was how Robert's old mate, Judy, acted. "What's Spike want to talk to me about?"

"I imagine it's about Whiskey. Have you thought what you're going to do with him?"

I'd been hopin' for a good solution, but everything I came up with was bad. "I was about to tell Whiskey he had to leave soon, when he said he was plannin' to go himself. I didn't think he was ready, so I convinced him to stay a couple more days."

"Crying shame about that poor pooch. But Taser, about our other problem, can I tell Spike you're coming to see him?"

"Sure. I'll get over there as soon as I can."

This was unusual for Spike. He hardly talked to other dogs and he didn't care much about me. So I couldn't help wondering...

What's up now?

TWENTY-ONE
New York City, July, 2007

Jody Carter rocked back in his lawn chair and pulled on his bottle of water. He was perched on a busy street curb, barely aware of the cars and trucks on Church Avenue behind him cruising by only feet from his head.

He looked down the long line of people stretching for blocks. Not everyone had brought chairs, some were sitting on blankets or standing on one leg, then the other. Even so, the feeling was festive and upbeat. American flags left hanging from the recent Fourth of July added to the party mood.

Jody pointed at the line of people and leaned over to his buddy. "Hey Craig. Wadda ya think. A hundred? Two hundred?"

Craig stood and looked down the line. "I'd say two hundred. You sure they open at six?"

"Yeah. They had to close at noon to stock the store."

Jody and Craig arrived with their water, lawn chairs and a huge bag of Doritos for sustenance. They got there at six in the morning, but they were still halfway down the line.

"I hope they got enough."

"Don't sweat it, we're covered."

They'd been sitting nine hours with only quick bathroom breaks to get them out of the chair. Most everyone else in line with them was dressed the same—shorts, T-shirt and sandals. Everyone, except for the well-mannered Asians with their collared shirts.

"You gonna get the four gig or the eight gig? Jody asked.

"Eight." Craig said. "Go big or go home. You?"

135

Jody mentally counted the hundred dollar bills in his pocket. "I don't have enough cash."

"Dude, you're crazy. You gotta get the eight gig model."

"Loan me the hundred, then."

"Yeah, right. It was tough enough coming up with what I got."

Jody went back to rocking in his lawn chair. He'd planned for this. He just didn't know if it was a good plan.

"I talked to the owner yesterday," Jody said. "I've already bought two Macbooks off the guy. He said he'd front me the extra cash 'til payday in exchange for this." Jody dug in his cargo-shorts pocket and pulled out a twenty-dollar gold piece and handed it to his friend.

Craig examined it closely, then he bit it with his front teeth. He looked for visible teeth marks. "Is this twenty-four carat?"

'I dunno. It's been in our family for years. My dad gave it to me. He said his dad gave left it to him, and maybe his dad before him, I forget."

"So aren't you gonna save it to your kid?"

"What kid? I'm never getting married," Jody said.

"Why buy the cow when…"

"Exactly. I don't wanna get saddled with a house and a kid. I mean, who do you know that gets married anymore?"

Craig nodded. "Too much responsibility. But the coin's probably worth something."

Jody shrugged. "It's old."

"Old, new, if that's twenty-four carat it's probably worth two iPhones."

"I can buy it back from him on Friday. At least this way I can get the right model."

Craig handed it back. "Good plan."

Jody put the 1933 Saint Gaudens coin back in his pocket and settled in for the final hours.

At six pm, the Apple Store reopened and the line rose and shuffled closer to the front door every few minutes. Now and then a customer would emerge from the store and hold his prized iPhone high to the sound of cheers from the crowd. It was a happening moment.

***

The happening wasn't lost on the two men watching from their black Ford Galaxy parked across the street. They looked at the Apple Store and the long line snaking inside.

"Lookit those frickin' idiots. All this over a damn phone."

Louie Morello leaned forward and peered through the dirty windshield. "What time they gonna close?"

"Midnight."

"No guard?"

"That's what Bobby said."

Guard or no guard, it didn't matter much to Louie, as long as the whole job didn't take over three minutes. He was the driver and knew time could be your friend or time could be your enemy. Three minutes was the limit, given police response time in that area of Brooklyn. Three minutes and ten seconds and he was gone.

Louie started the Ford and pulled away from the curb, its big V-8 rumbling impatiently under the hood. The car wasn't much to look at, but it ran like a bat out of hell. He blended seamlessly with the traffic and followed a Yellow Cab out of the area.

"Let's get some dinner at Angelina's. We got plenty of time."

At twenty minutes to midnight they were back, parked across the street from the Apple store, full of anticipation and a large serving of osso buco. The line into the store was shorter now but still boisterous.

"Bobby's gonna stay in the store bathroom past closin'. He'll be the last one out and let me in.

Louie nodded, only half-listening. The less he knew the better. The family didn't pay him to memorize details, only to drive the getaway car. He scanned the passing traffic for patrol cars, more out of out of habit than concern.

They watched the line and waited, but twelve o'clock came and went without the store closing its doors.

Now Louie grew nervous. "I thought you said midnight."

"Still too-many in line, I guess. Don't worry about it, it's just more cash in the till."

Louie opened the glove box and removed a roll of Tums, then ate two. He was too old for this crap anymore. A couple more jobs and he was through with the business. The times were changing. Ever since debit cards got popular, there usually wasn't enough cash on hand in most stores to balance the risk.

At thirty-five minutes past midnight the doors finally closed on the complaining crowd.

Nick Rossi opened the door and ambled over near the front of the Apple Store so he could be ready. When Bobby appeared and opened the door for Nick to go inside, Louie checked his watch.

He pulled the big Ford away from its spot down the street and stopped parallel to the store with the motor idling. He kept one eye on the door and one eye on his watch.

Two minutes.

Louie cursed, thinking they shoulda been out by then.

Two and a half.

VRROOOOMMM.

His right foot revved the motor unconsciously. What the hell were they doing?

CRACK!

CRACK!

Nick staggered out the door holding his side and a cloth bag. He fell into the back of the Ford and yelled.

"Go!"

Louie turned around. They had ten more seconds. "Where's Bobby?"

Nick gasped from the rear. "He's dead…undercover cop. Just go!"

138

In the reflected store lights Louie could see blood and a pained expression on his friend's face. This was not part of their plan.

Louie jerked the wheel sideways in front of a slow-moving delivery truck and floored it down Church Avenue. Angry horns and obscene gestures responded to his driving for the first mile, then he slowed and blended with the traffic. The garage was only four miles away. Louie kept checking his rear view, but it was a clean getaway. He stopped the car in the street, lifted the old wooden garage door and drove inside.

When he turned off the motor to listen for sirens, all he heard was the ticking of hot exhaust pipes cooling down. It was then he realized he'd heard nothing from the rear seat, certainly none of the usual driving complaints from Nick. No swearing—but no breathing, either. Just silence.

He turned around. "Hey Nick. You alright? Nick."

Louie got out of the front seat and opened the passenger door.

"Nick." He started to shake him but he knew from the first touch his friend was dead.

Louie ran his fingers through his graying hair.

Suddenly he had options open to him that he didn't have ten minutes ago. Options that were already in motion in his head.

Louie wiped down the steering wheel, dash and any surface where he might have left fingerprints. Then he left the body on the back seat, took the cloth bag and locked the car doors. He walked eight blocks to a dive hotel, thinking, planning.

At the desk, he paid the sleepy clerk cash from his pocket for one night, then walked up three flights to his room.

He set the robbery bag on the tiny bed and took off his shoes. Louie felt bad about his dead friend, but knew it could have been him just as easy.

Damn.

He'd never worried about dying before.

Must be gettin' old.

139

It was moments like this that confirmed his decision to leave the family. Finally, he had enough money to do just that.

He emptied the bag on the bed and started counting the cash, it took a few minutes. Then he counted again. It looked like nearly forty-thousand. If he added that to the rest of his stash he'd be set. But a move like this was not without high risk. Crossing Gambini wasn't smart. It was too bad the night's take wasn't higher.

At least it was all his.

He looked in the robbery bag to makes sure it was empty, and that's when he saw a single shiny gold coin in the bottom fold. He removed it and held it up to the light from his dim lamp bulb.

Probably a lucky coin for someone. Maybe the owner.

Louie had no idea if it was worth anything, but it was nice to have a souvenir from his last job.

He needed sleep, so he'd spend the night. In the early morning he'd get a train to Pittsburgh or Cleveland, then decide. On the trip he'd figure out a plan, but right now he needed to get out of the city. Either way, he was officially retired from the business.

He stretched out on the bed. The cash would last if he'd supplement it with an honest job. Maybe he'd be something like a cab driver or a delivery man. Something a little more fitting for his advancing age. And a change of scenery would be nice. He wanted to live someplace warmer in the winter. No snow.

Tucson, maybe.

Houses were cheap in Arizona. He could get a small home in the dry desert air and live out his years in peace. A small house with trees and a yard would be nice.

Oh yeah…and a dog. Always wanted one of them Dobermans.

TWENTY-ONE
Spike's House

Next mornin' I was stiff and sore, real sore. The bobcat's swipe got me worse than I thought. I limped around like Whiskey for a while, and then it felt a little better. What I needed was a walk to limber up.

So I figured it was a good time to visit Spike.

I waited some time after Robert left so the neighborhood would be empty. I didn't want to push my luck with Crenshaw or the dogcatcher. I headed out to the side gate and in a minute I was out. Meatloaf was sleepin' so I told Whiskey, just in case things went bad.

Normally I'd stop and see Winston when I was over close by, but I didn't wanna take the time. I only needed to know what Spike wanted, then I was gonna head home. The streets were empty so I felt good about gettin' back before Meatloaf even woke up.

When I turned down Spike's street, I saw him out in his usual spot, chained to the tree in the front yard. He was there most days, watchin' the house. Sometimes his master would sit out on the porch too, and Spike would lay next to him on the front patio. I think Winston said the master's name was Louie, Louie Smith.

Spike watched me approach, then nodded as I got close to him.

"Taser."

I noticed he didn't call me Blackie. I wasn't sure what that meant.

"Hey Spike. Winston said you wanted to talk to me."

"Yeah."

He looked around like he wasn't sure what to say. I almost thought he looked embarrassed, but that wouldn't be Spike.

"Look, Blackie...Taser, I know you and I don't see eye to eye all the time."

That was true. "You think I'm nosey. You think I snoop," I said.

"Yeah, I did say dat. 'Cause you are a snoop, but youse good at it."

I wasn't sure if that was a complement or not, but I didn't say anything.

"So," he continued. "If someone in da neighborhood's got a problem, youse da dog to see."

That much I took as a complement. "You need something?" I asked.

"I do. And you know most of it. You know we got pinched by some punk and his mutt."

"The dog didn't have anything to do with it. Whiskey just went along with his master."

"Be dat as it may, he's on my list. But dat's not da reason for dis meetin'. I'm askin' you ta help us. We gotta get dat coin back."

"What coin?"

"Da little bag on your friend's collar. It's got our coin in it."

"I thought it was jewelry. Female jewelry."

Spike shook his head. "No. It's just one gold coin. But dis coin is special. It's worth a million bones."

"A million? Why?"

"It's some special coin, don't ask me why. But if it gets out in da world and gets sold, it'll be in da news, then we're dead. Ya see, my master stole it when he lived back east."

"So he's worried about getting arrested by the police?"

"Nah. They can't pin dat rap on old Louie. He's worried about da family, dey got a long memory. He's been hiding from 'em. Dis coin was in with their take, it was their pinch. See, somebody wrote a big story in da New York newspapers about a rare coin taken in da robbery. Turns out dis coin is one of the only ones like it in the world."

"Family. You mean he took it from his family?"

"Not his blood, da mafia. You never hear a da mafia?"

"No.

"Back east, da mafia boys do mosta da crime. Mafia guys run things, keep stuff nice and orderly. My master useta drive a getaway car for 'em in snatch and grabs."

"So he's a criminal."

"Dat's a minor techna-callity. Besides, he's retired now. Plus, he never kilt nobody." Spike stepped closer. "He's a good human, Taser, just like your Robert. If dis coin business gets out, da family's gonna send a hitman to find my master and snuff him out. Me too, probably. It ain't a good idea ta cross dose mafia boys."

I understood now. Spike's master wasn't in witness protection like everyone thought, but he was hiding from some bad people just the same. I finally understood all the secrecy and Spike's behavior over the years.

"So you want me to find the coin," I said.

"Find it and bring it to me. I gotta make my master safe. I messed up and didn't stop dis robbery. I feel terrible about it." Spike's eyes were softer than I had ever seen. "Can you help us, Blackie? Please."

I nodded. There was nothing else I could say. "Yeah. I'll help you. I'll find the coin and return it."

But how I was gonna do that without getting killed was a mystery.

***

When I got home, Meatloaf was still sleepin', so I went out to tell Whiskey what Spike had said. I had to run it by someone in hopes of getting ideas. He listened to the whole story, then he got up and walked around the yard, not talkin'. His leg did seem better, but he limped bad. I was afraid he might always have that limp.

I told him what I thought. "The problem is the bobcat. The coin is probably under your tree just like I smelled, but so is the wildcat. If he ain't under there, he's close by hunting prey."

Whiskey stopped walking around and looked at me. "It looks like my master and I really messed things up. I'm sorry."

143

"It wasn't your fault."

"But I helped. And I lost the bag. There's only one thing to do. I've got to find the coin and return it myself."

"You? No way."

"I caused the problem so I've got to fix it. It's not your worry."

"Whiskey, you're not in any shape to go out there."

"It doesn't matter if I die or not. I've got no future. I know you can't find me a home, Meatloaf told me what the pack said. And if I go to the pound I'll end up dying there, so I might as well do the right thing."

This was goin' sideways on me quick. It would be canine suicide for Whiskey to try this. I couldn't let him do it.

He talked quickly, trying to convince me of his plan. "What if I go to the tree from the street side, not through the desert. I can walk along the big road and get to it that way."

I thought about that, it was a good idea and might work. But it was still risky. "What if the bobcat is there?"

"I can smell him before I get close. If he's under the tree, I'll come back."

He got me thinkin' serious, it wasn't a bad plan. It was actually the only plan that might work. If I couldn't stop him, maybe I could help him succeed.

"I could draw the bobcat away until you get the coin bag. You come back on the road and I'll come home through the park."

Whiskey brightened. "That would be great. When should we do this?"

"Tomorrow, I guess."

Just when I thought I had everything figured, the patio door opened and someone spoke.

What is this?

Catcrap.

It was Robert home early from work.

We were busted.

TWENTY-TWO
Caught in the Act

Robert stood there with this funny look on his face, tryin' to figure out Whiskey. Then he got down on one knee and called out.

Here boy.

Whiskey hobbled over and Robert stroked his head and talked nice to him. I got a little jealous but I didn't do nothin'. I figured Whiskey could use some love.

Where's your home, boy? You lost?

Robert found the wound on Whiskey's leg and looked closely at it. It musta been ok, because he didn't go get any of that magic tube stuff that helps you heal. Robert stood and walked over to the gate. He saw it was open, which was my fault. I shoulda closed it after goin' to Spike's.

Robert never comes home early, so I shouldn't have been too mad at myself, but I was. I sat there with a I-don't-know-nothin'-look, which must have worked. Robert shut the gate and looked at Whiskey like he was tryin' to decide what to do. Then he went in the house.

Whiskey looked at me. "Now what?"

I told him the truth. "I don't know what he's gonna do. At least he's not mad."

"I shoulda stayed in the dog house," Whiskey said, hangin' his head.

"Who'd have thought he'd be home early? Don't worry yet. I'm going inside and see what's up," I said.

I went in the dog door and bumped into Meatloaf. He was just about to come outside. We sat down in the laundry room to talk.

He had that guilty dog look. "I'm sorry, Taser. He caught me napping. I couldn't bark in time, he walked right out the back door."

"What's Robert doing home?" I asked.

"Probably waiting on a plumber human. Is the big white water dish plugged up?"

I walked into the little room and stuck my head in it and drank a little. "Seems normal to me. Why else would he come home early?"

"He coulda got fired from work."

"Nah. They love him there. Where is he, upstairs?"

"I don't know, he just left. He probably went back to work. What'd he say when he saw Whiskey?"

"Not much," I said. He probably thinks Whiskey came in the back yard because the side gate was open."

"Maybe he'll want to keep him," Meatloaf said.

"I hope not.' I said. Meat was worried there wouldn't be enough food to go around. I was worried there wouldn't be enough *love* to go around.

"So now what?"

"Wait until Robert does something. It's too bad, Whiskey and I came up with a good plan to find the lost coin."

"What lost coin?" Meatloaf asked.

I told him the story Spike told me. He listened carefully, then asked, "What's a mafia?"

"Spike says it's a pack of criminals."

"Oh great." Meatloaf sighed. "I told you I had a bad feeling about this."

He was right, but I didn't want to hear any of it.

Just then the front door opened and Robert came back in carrying a piece of paper. He went in the kitchen and picked up the telephone. We followed him in there and sat so we could listen better.

I cocked my head and lifted one ear.

Hello…found…lost…dog…tomorrow…night…9044…street…Scottsdale….

Catcrap.

"Oh no." I knew exactly what was up.

Meatloaf nudged me. "What? What's happening?"

146

I pointed with my snout. "You see that white thing he's holding?"

Meatloaf looked at the piece of paper in Robert's hand. "Yeah."

"That's the lost dog sign from the park. Robert just called the robber criminal to come get his lost dog."

"Whiskey?"

"Yeah. Robert just invited the robber to come to our house."

This was the worst possible thing I could have done. I had exposed my master to danger. Because of me, Robert invited a robber criminal into our very home.

I laid down on the floor and put my chin on my paws. I'd messed up before but this was bad. I whined like a lost puppy.

Hennngggg Hennngggg Hennngggg

***

Meatloaf tried to console me all afternoon but it wasn't workin'. Nothin' he said cheered me up.

"What if we get Whiskey to leave?" he asked.

I knew that wouldn't help. "The robber doesn't care about his dog, he only wants that coin. When he doesn't find it, he'll think Robert kept it."

"We could scare him off. Labradors can be scary." He thought about that a minute. "We can sound scary, anyway."

"Meat. He's got a gun. What if he shoots us? What if he shoots Robert with a gun bullet because he doesn't have the coin?"

Now Meatloaf was worried. "This is a mess. When's the robber coming over?"

"Tomorrow night."

"What if we get the pack to help us guard our house?"

I knew the only dog we could get would be Gizmo, and even a crazy Jack Russell wouldn't be enough. But there was one dog I knew who might scare a robber. "What about Harley?" I said.

147

Meatloaf liked that. "Yeah. He's real mean looking. And he bites good."

There was nothin' like a huge Rottweiler to scare humans. But the bite comment from Meatloaf reminded me of a problem. "That won't work. They watch him too close ever since he bit that human. They don't dare let Harley out of the house alone."

"What about the robber?"

"It's just you and me, buddy."

After that, I had to console Meatloaf.

***

Whiskey walked around the backyard, sniffing along the fence line and close to the house. The more he walked, the better his leg felt.

He wasn't happy about getting caught. It meant he'd have to leave the nice neighborhood and he didn't know where to go. Maybe Robert would call the dogcatcher and he'd get sent to the pound. He tried not to worry about it. He was most sad that he and Taser wouldn't be able to get the jewelry bag.

Whiskey stopped sniffing the yard and raised his head into the breeze. It was that smell off the desert again. He'd picked it up before, a gamey cat smell. He didn't say anything to Taser, but he thought the smell was the bobcat. It seemed to pass by twice a day on its hunting trips behind the subdivision.

Thinking about that gave Whiskey an idea.

All he had to do was get to the big Mesquite tree when the bobcat was at the other end of his hunting territory. He didn't need Taser's help. He could do it alone. He needed to fix the trouble he brought to Spike and his master.

The garbage truck would be coming through the neighborhood soon, probably tomorrow. He could slip out the gate when Robert took the big garbage can out before work. He'd seen it before when he considered leaving. He didn't want to leave without saying goodbye, but hopefully he'd be returning with the coin.

If not...

***

Robert was in and out a lot during the rest of the day. I thought maybe he had things to do around the house. It didn't happen often but I'd seen it before.

He messed around for a while in the front yard with tools and the hose faucet. He said something about plumbing. It must have been hard work, 'cause he kept callin' Funk for help, but that loser never came over to lend a hand. Then Robert did a little house cleaning—dog hair again—and he made some more telephone calls.

I lay on my back on the living room rug, thinking of ways to protect our house from the robber. I suppose it was possible the bad guy could only pickup Whiskey and leave, but he'd see right away the jewelry bag was off the collar. Then he'd get mad.

I tried to think of a way to get the police to come. That was their job, catchin' robbers. If I could just get police humans there tomorrow night, Robert would be safe.

Meatloaf walked in the room and stood lookin' down at me. "I heard Robert on the phone. We're getting a visitor."

I looked up from my spot on the rug. "Yeah, I'm tryin' to figure somethin' out."

Meatloaf shook his head. "No, I mean we're getting a visitor tonight. Shannon and Robert are going out to dinner. He told her to bring Rascal over for us to watch."

Great.

I was not in the mood for Shannon's hyper puppy. That also meant we probably weren't goin' to the park. That's double bad news.

Meatloaf motioned toward the backyard. "Did you tell Whiskey his master was coming over tomorrow?"

149

I hadn't. I didn't want Whiskey to end up goin' home with the robber. Maybe I was being selfish, but it didn't seem right. Anyway, I was hopin' the police would take the criminal away.

And I had an idea how to make it happen.

"Hey Meat. How about this. When the robber comes over and Robert lets him in, you and I and Whiskey will sneak out the side gate. We'll run over to Gizmo's place and bark like someone's gettin' murdered. I mean crazy barking and howlin'. Hopefully, a neighbor will call the police."

He sat down with a worried look on his face.. "You're gonna leave Robert right when he needs our protection?"

"We can't protect him from a bad guy with gun bullets. But if Whiskey is gone, the robber won't know his little bag is gone from the collar."

"I guess."

I admit it was weak, but how much can a Labrador do?

We were still trying to come up with a better idea when nighttime came and Shannon and Rascal arrived for their night out.

TWENTY-THREE
Double Trouble

The front door opened and Rascal ran in at full speed, panting in excitement. We sat in the hall and waited for him to run up.

He sniffed the floor a bit and then came over to us. "Hi Taser! Hi Mister Meat!"

"Hi kid."

It was then I saw Robert was dressed in his shiny shoes clothes like he wears to work. Shannon had some nice clothes on, too. I knew from bad experience this was not a good time to rub against their legs, so I kept my distance. For some reason they didn't seem to notice us.

Rascal ran out the dog door but I didn't follow him. I went in the kitchen with Robert to hear the talk. He said stuff to Shannon about finding Whiskey in the back and how he was that lost dog. He went to the big glass door and pointed out at Whiskey, but he didn't go out either.

Whiskey was walkin' around the back yard with Rascal following him—asking questions, probably.

Robert and Shannon didn't stay very long. Just before they went out to get in the Jeep, we got the usual lecture about being good dogs and woof woof woof. You know the story. I looked at him closely like I was payin' attention.

When we were finally alone, I still didn't go outside. I just stood looking out at Whiskey and Rascal. While I was standin' there, I had another idea.

I told Meatloaf. "I think we need to get Whiskey away from here. How about in the mornin', I open the gate and take him over to Winston's place to spend the night. I'd bet he could hide him."

151

Meatloaf got it. "So when the robber comes over, his dog will be gone."

"Or maybe, Robert when Robert sees Whiskey gone, he'll call off the meeting with the robber criminal."

"I like that plan better."

It was simple, really. No Whiskey, no problem.

"Maybe he should leave tonight," Meatloaf said.

I considered what that meant. "He won't have anywhere to stay. Let's wait until tomorrow so I can find a place." I felt bad enough about that.

Then Meatloaf raised the obvious point. "Taser. You're just postponing the inevitable. Whiskey is gonna end up in the pound. You gotta face it."

I couldn't, even though I knew Meat was right. The pound was too harsh a place for an injured dog. He'd be picked on by dog packs. "I don't want to think about that now."

"But…"

"No! Not yet!"

I padded over and looked out the big glass door. Whiskey and Rascal were lying on the patio talking, unaware of the dangers in the world.

***

When night came, the bobcat rose, stretched, and started his evening hunt. He walked with determination, purpose and a gnawing hunger. He would kill tonight, he would kill and eat.

He walked along the worn desert trail he now claimed as his own. This was his desert, the animals dwelling there belonged to him and he would take them when he chose.

He swung closer to the line of houses bordering the desert. He stopped at the first house he came to and sampled the night air. The evening's poultry dinner on the inside stove wafted out the open patio

152

door, then faded with its closing. He walked on, avoiding the homes with too-much noise or too-much activity.

In the past few days, all he had eaten was field mice. While they curbed his hunger somewhat, he wanted bigger game tonight.

He found it at a house with a huge black dog, but this dog was too formidable a threat by size alone. Even now, the dog sensed his presence and sounded his warning to stay away.

WOOF! WOOF! WOOF!

The bobcat moved to the two-story house next door and waited until the barking stopped.

He crouched on the desert floor and peered through the open fence, assessing the risk and the reward. At this house his chances were better. One dog was young, one dog was injured. Neither would be a threat or a challenge.

The wildcat settled in to wait for the right moment. He was in no hurry. There was no need to look further. He had found the evening's prey.

***

Meatloaf and I took over the television room while we waited for Robert and Shannon to come home. They left a movie on to keep us company and out of trouble. That was fine by me, I didn't want any more trouble than I had.

I watched the television for a while but my thoughts were somewhere else. I left Meat on the floor and went outside to check on Rascal and Whiskey.

They were still on the patio, talking.

I walked over. "What's up, dogs?"

Rascal panted with excitement. "Mister Whiskey is telling me stories about rescuing humans from burning houses!"

I looked at Whiskey and he shrugged. I decided it was doing him good and keeping Rascal out of trouble, so I left to go inside the house.

I started in the dog door, then stopped when I caught a whiff of something strange. For a moment I thought I smelled bobcat. I tensed and walked out close to the fence to check for danger. I tested the desert air as the faint scent came and went with the breeze. Finally I walked back to the house. I didn't see anything, but I couldn't be sure it was safe. I knew he walked past everyday, so catching his scent was normal. Still, I was jumpy.

"Rascal! Time to come inside."

"Please Mister Taser. Just one more story."

"Just one." With that, I went in the house.

Meatloaf was exactly where I left him, lying on his side, staring out into space.

"Whadda you doin'?" I asked

"I'm working with numbers in my head."

"How's that goin'?"

"Not good. If they bring home two doggie bags, but we have four dogs here, how much food does that leave?"

I didn't answer him, I just stood there, strainin' to hear.

Meatloaf saw me acting strange. "Everything alright?" he asked.

I stood on the kitchen tile, my head turned slightly. My tail straightened, then stiffened. "Somethin' doesn't feel right."

Meatloaf raised his head but didn't get up. I padded quietly into the living room to look around. The hairs on my back stood up as I crouched slightly. It all looked normal, but I knew it wasn't. Something was wrong.

Woof.

I barked quietly, then listened.

Woof.

BANG!

The front door flew open and a huge human bolted in. He shut the broken door behind him and looked around the room, barely glancing at me. His clothes stunk like Robert does after runnin' and his hair was kinda wild and messy. He had one hand in his pocket, but when he saw me he took it out. He was holding a black gun.

I knew who this was.

Urrrrrrrgh.

A growl rolled out through curled lips. I wanted to bite this man in the worst way. He was an intruder in my home.

Urrrrrrrgh.

SHUTUP, he told me.

I watched him walk down the hall and into the kitchen, so I followed a few steps behind, growling the whole way. He told me to shutup again, but I wasn't gonna obey him. Meatloaf was on the floor over by the television with his chin on his front paws. His eyes followed the robber as he walked around the kitchen. The robber called out.

Whiskey!

He waited, then walked to the rear windows. He looked, saw Whiskey and opened the big glass door.

Whiskey! Come here!

Whiskey slinked over and came inside the house.

I was standing behind the robber, and I gave Rascal a look that said go away. He ran to the side yard.

The man bent down and grabbed Whiskey's collar. He looked on one side and then the other. Then he pulled Whiskey close to his face, still holding his collar.

Where is it?

He stood up angrily and yelled again in a way I hadn't heard since my first mean master. Whiskey hung his head and looked down. Another growl came out of me without thinkin'.

Urrrrrrrgh.

He ignored me and looked down at Whiskey.

Damn dog.

Urrrrrrrgh.

He didn't pay any attention to me, he was busy looking around the room. He set his gun on the kitchen counter and started opening

155

drawers and searching through them. He tossed aside the papers and little stuff in his way. Some of it ended up on the floor as he searched. He looked in every drawer in all the rooms, and then he took his gun with him and went upstairs.

Meatloaf got up and came over by me. "Is that the robber?"

"Gotta be," I said. "He came tonight to surprise us. Robert thinks he's comin' tomorrow."

"The guy fooled everybody."

I looked at Whiskey. "You alright?"

He nodded but didn't say anything, but I was sure he felt terrible.

"He's mad," Meatloaf said. "He wants that coin."

"I'm glad Robert isn't here. He might be mean to him."

Whiskey looked up. "He's not gonna leave without that coin. He'll wait for Robert to come home."

I didn't want to hear that, but I knew Whiskey was right.

"We should get away," Meatloaf said. "The front door is open."

I looked and saw wood splinters on the door. It was hanging partly open. "We can't leave Robert. We can't leave Rascal."

I looked up the stairs. I could hear the robber up there tossing things around, probably searching for the coin bag. But Meat was right about one thing.

"We hafta do somethin'," I said, then realized it was too late. The big garage door banged and groaned and started to open. Robert was home.

We tried to warn him.

BOW WOW WOW

WOOF WOOF WOOF

RUFF RUFF RUFF

We all barked so much that Harley the Rottweiler started barking next door. Then Robert came in.

Taser! Meatloaf! Be quiet.

Robert and Shannon walked in the hall and looked around, then into the kitchen. He looked at the open drawers and the stuff on the floor and then us. He musta known it was a robbery 'cause he picked up the phone.

Yes, I thought. Call the police!

But then the robber came in the room pointing his pistol.

Put the phone down.

Robert did.

Where is it?

Robert and Shannon were standing together in the kitchen while the robber was in the hall. They didn't answer.

Where's the coin! He looked mad.

Robert looked scared, and I couldn't blame him. I woulda been scared myself but I was too angry with myself.

What coin?.

The coin in the bag.

Robert looked at Shannon, then back. *What bag?*

The robber pointed at Whiskey, who was trying to make himself very small on the kitchen floor. *The bag that was hanging on his collar.*

Now Robert didn't look scared, only confused. How could he be in trouble for something he didn't know anything about?

I don't know what you're talking about. There was no bag on his collar.

The robber held his pistol up and pointed it right at Robert.

You're lying. I ain't leavin' without it.

I gathered my legs under me so I could rush the robber and bite his leg.

But Whiskey beat me to it. He rushed forward and clamped onto the robber's leg with his teeth. The robber swore and tried to shake Whiskey off. Whiskey hung on, growling like a rabid dog.

Rrrrrrrrrrrrrrrrrrrr Rrrrrrrrrrrrrrrrrrrrr Rrrrrrrrrrrrrrrrrrrr

Just then I heard a pitiful howl from the back yard, part cry for help and part scared puppy.

YEEEEEEAAAAAAOOOOOOOWWWWWWWLLLL

My head jerked up. Rascal!

I didn't know what to do. I didn't want to leave my master in trouble, but Rascal's cry sounded awful.

YEEEEEEAAAAAAOOOOOOWWWWWWWLLLL

That was all I could take. I ran to the dog door. POW! I blew right through, then realized Meatloaf was followin' behind me. We ran to the backyard, but I knew from the smell right away what was wrong.

Bobcat!

It had Rascal trapped behind Robert's wheelbarrow against the fence. Rascal was huggin' the ground and wimperin' awful, tryin' to stay out of reach.

Meatloaf and I spread out, trapping the wildcat between us. He crouched and hissed, flexing his muscles, ready to fight.

BOW WOW WOW WOOF WOOF WOOF BOW WOW WOW

We barked because that's what we do, but I knew we weren't gonna get rid of this killer without a fight. He looked at me and then at Meatloaf, still crouched and poised to jump one of us. I moved sideways, hopin' to get him to go after me and not Meatloaf.

I'd only get one good bite. I had to bite his head and kill him quick. I tensed for the fight, but then I heard explosions in the house.

BOOM! BOOM!

Gun bullets, it had to be. The robber shot my master!

I didn't know what to do. The bobcat hissed and stared directly at me, ready to pounce. I had to do it, now!

Meatloaf barked.

Harley barked.

Rascal cried.

Somebody shot a gun.

BOOM!

The bobcat crumpled to the ground in a pile and didn't move. I stared at it, then turned around. Shannon stood on our patio in her high heels, pointing a gun right at the dead bobcat. She walked closer, still pointing her gun. She walked over and kicked the cat with one foot, then put the gun down and called to her puppy.

Here Rascal.

Rascal ran out from behind the wheelbarrow and into Shannon's arms. She hugged him close.

Robert stepped out of the house with the phone at his head. I looked at Meatloaf and he looked back at me.

It was over.

TWENTY-FOUR
After.

We all went inside the house. The robber was gone, all that was left of his visit was the mess he made on the floor and two bullet holes in the hall wall.

I sniffed the air, it smelled like burnt something.

"What happened in here?" Meatloaf asked.

I didn't know. I looked up and saw Shannon put her little gun back in her little purse.

Rascal saw her put the gun away, too. "That's her clock," he said. "She keeps it by her bed at night and in her purse during the day."

Then I understood. It wasn't a clock. It was a Glock.

Robert talked to the police on the phone a while, then we all sat around and waited. I thought they would clean up the mess on the floor, but they didn't. Robert had two beers, but Shannon just drank water.

Suddenly there were all these flashing lights out front. Meat and I ran out the dog door and looked through the gate.

Woof Woof

"Cops are here," Meat said.

We ran back inside so we didn't miss anything.

A couple Scottsdale police humans came to the door and Robert let them in. They looked all over the house and looked at the dead bobcat and the bullet holes in the wall. There was a lot of talkin' and writin' on papers, during which we got bored because nobody paid us any attention.

The one I felt sorry for was Whiskey, because his master ran away and abandoned him. It was bad enough havin' a bad master, but it's tougher yet when even he doesn't want you. Whiskey just curled up in a little ball on the floor and looked pathetic.

I went over to him. "I'm sorry, Whiskey."

"He just left me." He looked up with sad eyes. "He never cared about me, did he?"

I lied to him. "I'm sure he did, he didn't want to get caught." Or shot, I thought. "What happened when we went outside?"

He sighed. "All I know is, I was biting my master on the leg, and he was swinging me around and hitting me to get me off, and then I heard those loud noises. It scared me so much I let go of his leg. Then he ran out the front door."

"You saved us, Whiskey," I said. "You and Shannon."

Whiskey didn't say anything. He was probably sad about not havin' a home.

I was sad myself. I didn't know what was gonna happen to him.

The police finally left, and suddenly more beer came out of the cold box. Robert and Shannon sat on the couch and drank beer and talked.

Meat and Whiskey and Rascal and I all went to sleep on the floor. We'd had enough fun for one night.

***

The next mornin' was a rubber shoe day, so Robert didn't hafta go to work. He got up early and cleaned up the rest of the mess the robber made. Then he came in the hall and stared at the two gun bullet holes in the wall and shook his head.

I didn't want Robert to fix the holes. They looked kinda cool.

Whiskey spent the night outside in the doghouse, even though I told him he could sleep in the house with us. I think he still felt bad.

After Robert had some burnt water and oats cereal, he went outside and got rid of the dead bobcat. He tossed the body and a shovel over the fence into the desert, then he climbed over himself. Meat and I watched from the backyard.

161

Robert walked out in the desert almost to the sandwash and dug a hole with his shovel, just like he does when he puts plants in the ground. But this time he planted the bobcat. Then he covered it all up good. Then he came back and climbed over our fence.

"Is that what they do when you die?" Meatloaf asked.

It looked kinda sad. "I hope not."

"You'd think they'd wait until you got all flat and dried out, like those dead cats you see on the road."

"I love those flat cats."

I thought it was better to plant the bobcat so we didn't hafta look at until it got dry

That only left Whiskey to deal with.

Robert went in the little room and washed his hands, then came back outside. He grabbed chair and we all sat on the patio in the sun. He looked at Whiskey and then called him over to pet him. When we saw what was goin' on we went over and got some pats, too.

Robert stared at Whiskey a long time, then out across the desert. When he picked up the phone I knew it was over for our friend. But for some reason, Robert never made the phone call to Animal Control. He just sat there holdin' the phone.

Pretty soon he got up and went to the drawer where we keep the leashes. He put one on Meatloaf and one on me, then he put another one on Whiskey. It looked like a park trip to me, which was good, since we missed a trip the night before.

We fought for first position at the door, but I muscled my way to the front and pulled on my leash down the walk. Robert held on tight to all three dogs as we walked down the sidewalk and past Crenshaw's place. He kept us on a leash at the park while we walked around and sniffed and pooped and peed.

You know, the usual dog stuff.

But then Robert did something unusual. He tied Meatloaf and me to the sign post at the park, but he didn't tie Whiskey. Robert held his finger up like he does when he wants our attention, and said:

162

Stay.

Then he took Whiskey and started walkin' home. I just watched him walk away, my head cocked, my brain thinkin'. Whiskey was right at his side, limping along somethin' terrible.

"Where's Robert going?" Meat asked.

"I dunno."

We watched him go back toward our house, but then stop and go up old man Crenshaw's walk. He went right up to Crenshaw's front door and knocked.

"Now what?"

The door opened and old man Crenshaw looked at Robert and then Whiskey. Whiskey sat on the stoop and hung his head. Robert talked to Crenshaw for a while, and then they walked away. Crenshaw watched from his open door.

"What's happening?" asked Meatloaf. "Is Robert blaming everything on Whiskey?"

"I don't think so," I said. "Robert asked him something, but I guess Mister Crenshaw said no."

When Robert was almost at the sidewalk, Crenshaw called out. Then he came out of his house with a stick.

"Catcrap!" Meatloaf backed up. "He's gonna beat Whiskey!"

Crenshaw started toward Whiskey with his stick. But then I saw Crenshaw was walking with a limp, too. He used the stick to help him walk. He went right up to Whiskey, then bent over and talked to him nicely and stroked his head. When he straightened up, he reached for Whiskey's leash and smiled at Robert.

Thank you, Crenshaw said. *I'll take good care of him.*

Then they limped along together and went inside the house, a sad old man and his sad old dog.

Maybe now, I thought, they won't be sad anymore.

EPILOGUE
Two days later…Monday Morning

It was sometime after breakfast when I finally made it back out to the desert. This time I was enjoying the sunshine and not worried about the bobcat. When I remembered his hole, I walked over to where he was planted. I saw the fresh pile of dirt and slowed, then went right up, sniffing the ground.

Yes.

Satisfied he was still there and still dead, I continued on my way down the trail, dodging the scary jumping cactus. In not much time I was at the big Mesquite tree. I stopped and stared at it, still cautious from the overpowering scent of bobcat.

I stepped closer and looked through the thick branches, then ducked under them and into the lair. The bobcat's musky scent was almost too much, but I had to separate the smells to find the coin bag. I sniffed and pawed at the ground until I got a hint of leather.

I pawed at one spot, hopeful I'd found it—but there was nothin' there.

Maybe the bobcat ate it.

I kept pushing aside dead leaves and grass, sniffing as I moved all around. Finally, I had to admit it wasn't under the tree. Maybe it had been one time, maybe not.

I walked out from under the branches—and then I saw it. It was hangin' in the air from a low branch. I figured Whiskey must have snagged his collar on the branch and it pulled the bag off.

I put my mouth on the bag and pulled it free. It was soft on the outside and hard on the inside. Whatever it was, I didn't want to lose it, so I clamped shut. I turned and walked quickly along the trail out of the desert.

I walked right past my house all the way to Spike's street. I had to drop the bag and pant a few times, but I made it in good time.

Spike was out in the front, watchin' the street as usual. I walked right up to him and dropped the coin bag at his feet. He sniffed it, then looked up.

"Blackie. Dis is it!"

"Yeah."

"How'd youse find it?"

"The usual," I said. "Snoopin'. Meddlin'."

Spike nodded. "Like I said, you're good at it. Was it under that tree?"

"Kinda. You sure that's it?"

"Oh yeah. We had dis thing a long time."

"What are you gonna do with it now? A million dollars is a lot of money."

He seemed to consider that. "Money don't mean nothin' if you're dead. Dis coin just brings us big trouble. Maybe I'll dig a hole and bury it in da back yard."

"But your master…"

"He'll think it's gone. Only now we'll be safe."

I realized he was right. The important thing was keeping it secret. "Whatever you think, Spike."

"So. How can I repay ya?"

That much I knew. "You can leave Whiskey alone. He's gonna be livin' in the neighborhood now."

"Yeah. Winston told me." Spike shook his head. "Old man Crenshaw. Who'd a thought?"

Not me. "So. We got a deal?"

"Deal. Whiskey's off my list." He picked up the bag and moved toward the backyard. Before he got there he put it down and looked back at me.

"Hey Blackie. Uhh, thanks."
I nodded and started back home.
No problem. Just doin' my job.

THE END

Follow the Howl Series at:
www.ahowlinthenight.com

A Howl in the Night
The Twilight Howl
A Howl for Help

The PG youth version of A Howl in the Night is available as:
The Midnight Howl

Other books by JK Brandon:
The Kennedy Rifle
The Steel Violin
A Kind Word and a Gun

The following is a sample chapter from
A Howl in the Night

ONE

As soon as I heard it, I knew something was terribly wrong.

It was long, low, and mournful, like a little hound heart was broken and nothing would ever make it right. A thousand hairs on my back stood straight up. Even Meatloaf woke up, and nothing wakes him up.

He thought it was the wind whistling through our wood-slat gate. It was the hot time, and sometimes dust storms blow in out of nowhere, like tonight. But I knew this was a different animal altogether.

I cocked my head like some mutts do when they don't get it, except I knew exactly what was up. Just then a big wind gust slammed the house, blowin' a bunch of seed pods out of our Mesquite tree and sending them raining down all over the patio.

That was it.

We bounced off the living room rug and bolted for the backyard. Pow! I blew the dog door at full speed, Meatloaf clippin' my heels. We stopped and went rigid out on the grass, straining to hear through the storm. The wind raised and rustled the long hairs of my black coat. I took a step forward and listened harder, desperate for a clue. Then it came again.

Woooooooooooooooooooooooooooooooooooooooooooooooooooooo.

I shivered, even in the warm breeze.

It was Nelly, the little Beagle three-houses down. I'd heard her howl before, but not like this. Never. That's when I knew somethin' awful must have happened.

168

We looked helplessly at each other, there was nothing we could do, Nelly was three houses away. That's three yards with tall block fences and wood-slat gates as tight as a chain choke collar at full yank. Meatloaf let loose a couple of mean, rumbling barks, hoping to scare off whatever might be menacing the neighborhood. I did a quick perimeter check, ears up and nose to the ground. I nodded at my partner. The yard was clear.

Harley next door started with his baritone bark, then Roxie down the street, except her squeak wouldn't scare away a mouse. All around the neighborhood, dogs spoke up to warn the unwary—not at my house.

Meatloaf stood by my side. "Whadda ya think?"

I had my nose in the air, searching for tell-tale scents. "I don't like it. Smells like trouble comin' our way."

We ducked as a white light streaked past our house and flashed down the street, then streaked by once again.

Police-humans.

We dashed to the gate and stuck our noses through the slats. Best as I could smell, there was a lone female-cop at Nelly's place. Somebody must have called the police, probably that old busy-body across the street from us. She didn't sleep much, except during the day when we wanted to bark at cats.

Ghhetricmmspdpvkjfresjjttheehhsk.

A two-way cackled with cop talk in the night air, bouncing off the neighbor's house and funneling into our backyard. I knew a lot of human words, but I couldn't make any sense of this babble. No matter, I thought I knew what was up.

"Gotta be a burglary," I said.

Roxie was still barkin' on and off, and of course Harley the Rottweiler wouldn't shut up. Neither would that radio.

Kfjkfhjwurirnchdjdotiwmerhddhh.

We ran to the other side of the yard, but nothin' was shaking so we hustled back to our gate. I was gettin' nervous, the police shoulda been out of there by now.   It was startin' to look bad for the Nelly household.

"Here comes another one," said Meatloaf.

There were two more, actually. Now we had three cop cars and two light bars strobing our street.   It'd be different if this was Saturday night at the Deuce, but this was Scottsdale, baby.   Nothin' bad ever happens up here.

"What about the police?" he asked.

I sniffed deep. "The female's still inside, but now there's four males out beatin' the bushes."

"Don't know, dawg, that's a lot of police for a burglary."

Meat was right.   That many cops in one place usually meant a beer bust or a body turning cold. Even in this heat.

Then it hit me.   The scent was faint, very faint—then all too strong. It floated over on the thick night-air when the wind died, invading my strongest sense.   I stepped to one side and threw up.   Meat couldn't smell it, but watching me retch, he knew what made me puke.

Blood.

"Woof Woof! Woof Woof!"

Meatloaf let 'em have it again.   That started another round in the neighborhood, so I joined the chorus.

"Bow Wow Wow Wow!"

That felt great—until we got the word from the man.

Taser! Meatloaf! Get in here.

Busted.

Robert held the door open and waited for us. He had that face on.

No barking.

Heads hanging, we trudged back inside.   I don't know if Robert heard the police but he didn't miss our warning.   He told us again to shut it, then he turned out the light and went upstairs.   It looked like the block party was over.   Pretty soon it was as still and quiet as a pooch on the way to the vet.

170

Meatloaf plopped down on the carpet and went right out. He was snoring in no time, but I couldn't get poor Nelly out of my mind. Her sad howl reminded me of a bad affair and a hapless hound I've tried to forget. I put my chin on my paws and stared out into the darkness, thankful for my master and the roof over our heads.

When sleep finally came, my tired paws twitched and jerked to that same nightmare, that same horror, that same moment.

***

My eyes popped open at first light, but I lay there a while and analyzed the action at Nelly's. I tried to find a good side, but every way I flipped it, it came up trouble. Meatloaf and I know all about trouble, we been around the block before. We didn't just fall off the animal-control wagon.

By the way, we're Labs.

Black Labs.

Meatloaf was still sleeping, but I got up and stretched my legs. It seemed like it was brighter outside, which was a good thing, first-food would be coming up quick. I heard Robert moving around upstairs—heavy footsteps, water splashing, doors closing—stuff like that.

I was gettin' impatient, I wanted the day to get rolling. I'd have gone upstairs to see what the holdup was, but that's a big "No-No, Bad Dog" around here. But it was time to go, even Meatloaf started to stir from his spot on the carpet.

The noise upstairs got louder, so me and Meatloaf moved to the bottom of the stairs to whine and wait. When you're a dog, you spend most of your life waiting. Waiting for food. Waiting for pats. Waiting for a walk. If you're Meatloaf that's no problem, you just plop down and rest. Me, I gotta move.

So I left him huggin' the floor and went to see what was happening out front. I nosed the window shutter open and right away I spotted a rabbit sittin' in the yard. That just made me crazy, but I chilled. Those

171

rabbits sit there like a statue and think we can't see 'em. Spottin's not the problem, catchin's the tough part.

I turned my head and saw a couple black and white cars down the street. At least that's the color I thought they were, because I got dog's eyes, and they stink during the day. According to the Animal Channel, we see shades of grey, washed-out yellows and blues—but no red or green.

A bark rumbled deep in my throat, but I choked it off. I didn't like these cop cars in my neighborhood, but I didn't want to make a fuss before we got something to eat. Sometimes you gotta stay focused.

Hi, guys!

It was Robert. He came down the stairs and rubbed our bellies while we rolled around on the floor like a couple of idiots. Robert went out to get the papers so I followed along to check things out. The rabbit outside was long gone, no surprise to me. The minute you get close to those long-eared rats they disappear like a dropped grape rolling by Meatloaf's nose.

Robert snagged the papers and glanced down the street at the black and whites. I wanted him to go check it out, but he went back inside to feed us, so I didn't wanna complain. I get a little nervous if I don't get my food first-thing, 'cause you never know if they're gonna forget you. Sometimes humans get their priorities screwed up.

So we got a couple cups of dry Eukanuba in separate bowls. I got the performance blend, Meat got the weight-control type. I don't much care for it; neither does my buddy, but he'll eat anything. I scarfed my chow down in a hurry so he couldn't steal any, then we hit the water dish for slurp and burp.

That's when the doorbell rang.

Normally we bark like crazy at the door bell, but I kinda expected this visit so I gave Meatloaf the look. I've seen these black and white cars before. I saw plenty of them during my time on the Westside; they bring cops in dark-gray uniforms with lots of questions. This morning I wanted to hear those questions.

172

I've learned a lot of human words in my time. It's not that unusual for a dog, not like a mutt opening a door or using a fork. I'm beyond all the normal words—eat, park, treat, stay—every hound knows those and more. Some dogs know a lot more, like me. You just gotta listen, these humans know some stuff.

We sat perfectly still in the living room so Robert wouldn't lock us up in the garage, but I put both ears up when they started talking. I picked out the human words I knew.

Good............Scottsdale.Police............hear............noise......
...killed.......neighbor............call.........anything...

Pretty soon I can't help it myself, I started pacing back and forth and whining.

Heeennnnnggg. Heeennnnnggg. Heeennnnnnnnnnnnnnnggg.

Robert pointed his finger at me.

Taser! Hush!

I needed to tell them about Nelly's howl last night, but they wouldn't listen to me. I don't get why they can't understand my words. I think it's a lip problem, their little human lips open and close real tight when their words come out. Me and Meatloaf, our lips don't close real good, they just kinda hang there, sloppy-like.

The cops finally left. Too bad, we didn't learn squat from that visit, it looked like we had to wait for dogs-at-dusk, our nightly mutt-meeting down at the park. If anyone knows what's goin' down around here, it's the neighborhood dogs.

Made in the USA
San Bernardino, CA
16 January 2013